悅讀
莎士比亞
四大喜劇故事

作者_ Charles and Mary Lamb

仲夏夜之夢
威尼斯商人
皆大歡喜
第十二夜

目錄

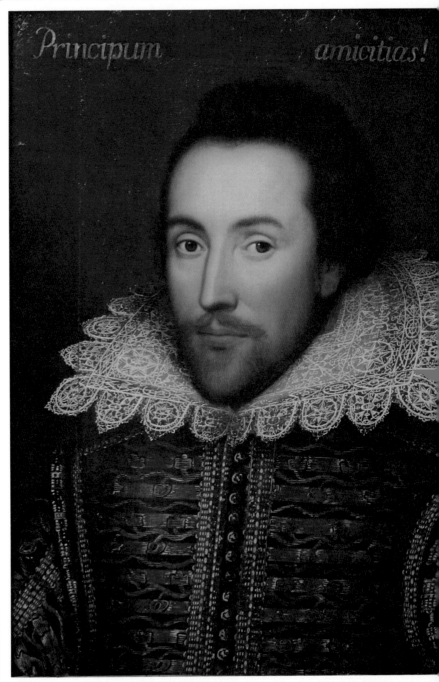

威廉·莎士比亞（William Shakespeare, 1564–1681）

莎士比亞二三事

威廉・莎士比亞（William Shakespeare）出生於英國的史特拉福（Stratford-upon-Avon）。莎士比亞的父親曾任地方議員，母親是地主的女兒。莎士比亞對婦女在廚房或起居室裡勞動的描繪不少，這大概是經由觀察母親所得。他本人也懂得園藝，故作品中的植草種樹表現鮮活。

1571 年，莎士比亞進入公立學校就讀，校內教學多採拉丁文，因此在其作品中到處可見到羅馬詩人奧維德（Ovid）的影子。當時代古典文學的英譯日漸普遍，有學者認為莎士比亞只懂得英語，但這種說法有可議之處。舉例來說，在高登的譯本裡，森林女神只用 Diana 這個名字，而莎士比亞卻在《仲夏夜之夢》一劇中用奧維德原作中的 Titania 一名來稱呼仙后。和莎士比亞有私交的文學家班・強生（Ben Jonson）則曾說，莎翁「懂得一點拉丁文，和一點點希臘文」。

莎士比亞的劇本亦常引用《聖經》典故，在伊麗莎白女王時期，通俗英語中已有很多《聖經》詞語。此外，莎士比亞應該很知悉當時年輕人所流行的遊戲娛樂，當時也應該有巡迴劇團不時前來史特拉福演出。 1575 年，伊麗莎白女王來到郡上時，當地人以化裝遊行、假面戲劇、煙火來款待女王，《仲夏夜之夢》裡就有這種盛會的描繪。

莎士比亞出生地：史特拉福（Stratford-upon-Avon）

環球劇場（Globe Theatre）（1997 年重建）

1582 年，莎士比亞與安‧海瑟威（Anne Hathaway）結婚，但這場婚姻顯得草率，連莎士比亞的雙親都因不知情而沒有出席婚禮。1586 年，他們在倫敦定居下來。1586 年的倫敦已是英國首都，年輕人莫不想在此大展抱負。史特拉福與倫敦之間的交通頻仍，但對身無長物的人而言，步行仍是最平常的旅行方式。伊麗莎白時期的文學家喜好步行，1618 年，班‧強生就曾在倫敦與愛丁堡之間徒步來回。

莎士比亞初抵倫敦的史料不充足，有諸多揣測。其中一説為莎士比亞曾在律師處當職員，因為他在劇本與詩歌中經常提及法律術語。但這種説法站不住腳，因為莎士比亞多有訛用，例如他在《威尼斯商人》和《一報還一報》中提到的法律原理和程序，就有諸多錯誤。事實上，伊麗莎白時期的作家都喜歡引用法律詞彙，這是因為當時的文人和律師時有往來，而且中產階級也常介入訴訟案件，許多法律術語自然為常人所知。莎士比亞樂於援用法律術語，這顯示了他對當代生活和風尚的興趣。莎士比亞自抵達倫敦到告老還鄉，心思始終放在戲劇和詩歌上，不太可能接受法律這門專業領域的訓練。

莎士比亞在倫敦的第一份工作是劇場工作。當時常態營業的劇場有兩個：「劇場」（the Theatre）和「帷幕」（the Curtain）。「劇場」的所有人為詹姆士‧波比奇（James Burbage），莎士比亞就在此落腳。「劇場」財務狀況不佳，1596 年波比奇過世，把「劇場」交給兩個兒子，其中一個兒子便是著名的悲劇演員理查‧波比奇（Richard Burbage）。後來「劇場」因租約問題無法解決，決定將原有的建築物拆除，在泰晤士河的對面重建，改名為「環球」（the Globe）。不久，「環球」就展開了戲劇史上空前繁榮的時代。

伊麗莎白時期的戲劇表演只有男演員，所有的女性角色都由男性擔任。演員反串時會戴上面具，效果十足，不損故事的意境。莎士比亞本身也是一位出色的演員，曾在《皆大歡喜》和《哈姆雷特》中分別扮演忠僕亞當和國王鬼魂這兩個角色。

莎士比亞很留意演員的說白，這點可從哈姆雷特告誡伶人的對話中窺知一二。莎士比亞熟稔劇場的技術與運作，加上他也是劇場股東，故對劇場的營運和組織都甚有研究。不過，他的志業不在演出或劇場管理，而是劇本和詩歌創作。

1591 年，莎士比亞開始創作戲劇，他師法擅長喜劇的約翰‧李利（John Lyly），以及曾寫下轟動一時的悲劇《帖木兒大帝》（*Tamburlaine the Great*）的克里斯多夫‧馬婁（Christopher Marlowe）。莎翁戲劇的特色是兼容並蓄，吸收各家長處，而且他也勤奮多產。一直到 1611 年封筆之前，每年平均寫出兩部劇作和三卷詩作。莎士比亞慣於在既有的文學作品中尋找材料，又重視大眾喜好，常能讓平淡無奇的作品廣受喜愛。

在當時，劇本都是賣斷給劇場，不能再賣給出版商，因此莎劇的出版先後，並不能反映其創作的時間先後。莎翁作品的先後順序都由後人所推斷，推測的主要依據是作品題材和韻格。他早期的戲劇作品，無論悲劇或喜劇，性質都很單純。隨著創作的手法逐漸成熟，內容愈來愈複雜深刻，悲喜劇熔冶一爐。

自 1591 年席德尼爵士（Sir Philip Sidney）的十四行詩集發表後，十四行詩（sonnets，另譯為商籟）在英國即普遍受到文人的喜愛與仿傚。其中許多作品承續佩脫拉克（Petrarch）的風格，多描寫愛情的酸甜苦樂。莎士比亞的創作一向很能反應當時的文學風尚，在詩歌體裁鼎盛之時，他也將才華展現在十四行詩上，並將部分作品寫入劇本之中。

莎士比亞的十四行詩主要有兩個主題：婚姻責任和詩歌的不朽。這兩者皆是文藝復興時期詩歌中常見的主題。不少人以為莎士比亞的十四行詩表達了他個人的自省與懺悔，但事實上這些內容有更多是源於他的戲劇天分。

1595 至 1598 年，莎士比亞陸續寫了《羅密歐與茱麗葉》、《仲夏夜之夢》、《馴悍記》、《威尼斯商人》和若干歷史劇，他的詩歌戲劇也在這段時期受到肯定。當時的法蘭西斯 · 梅爾斯（Francis Meres）就將莎士比亞視為最偉大的文學家，他說：「要是繆思會説英語，一定也會喜歡引用莎士比亞的精彩語藻。」「無論是悲劇或喜劇，莎士比亞的表現都是首屈一指。」

闊別故鄉十一年後，莎士比亞於 1596 年返回故居，並在隔年買下名為「新居」（New Place）的房子。那是鎮上第二大的房子，他大幅改建整修，爾後家道日益興盛。莎士比亞大筆的固定收入主要來自表演，而非劇本創作。當時不乏有成功的演員靠演戲發財，甚至有人將這種現象寫成劇本。除了表演，劇場行政和管理的工作，以及宮廷演出的賞賜，都是他的財源。許多文獻均顯示，莎士比亞是個非常關心財富、地產和社會地位的人，讓許多人感到與他的詩人形象有些扞格不入。

伊麗莎白女王過世後，詹姆士一世（James I）於 1603 年登基，他把莎士比亞所屬的劇團納入保護。莎士比亞此時寫了《第十二夜》和佳評如潮的《哈姆雷特》，成就傲視全英格蘭。但他仍謙恭有禮、溫文爾雅，一如十多前年初抵倫敦的樣子，因此也愈發受到大眾的喜愛。

史特拉福聖三一教堂（Holy Trinity Church）
的莎翁紀念雕像和莎翁之墓

從這一年起，莎士比亞開始撰寫悲劇《奧賽羅》。他寫悲劇並非是因為精神壓力或生活變故，而是身為一名劇作家，最終目的就是要寫出優秀的悲劇作品。當時他嘗試以詩入劇，在《哈姆雷特》和《一報還一報》中尤其爐火純青。隨後《李爾王》和《馬克白》問世，一直到四年後的《安東尼與克麗奧佩脫拉》，寫作風格登峰造極。

1609 年，倫敦瘟疫猖獗，隔年，莎士比亞決定告別倫敦，返回史特拉福退隱。1616 年，莎士比亞和老友德雷頓、班・強生聚會時，可能由於喝得過於盡興，回家後發高熱，一病不起。他將遺囑修改完畢後，恰巧在他 52 歲的生日當天去世。

七年後，昔日的劇場友人收錄他的劇本，編輯全集出版，包括喜劇、歷史劇、悲劇等共 36 部。此書不僅不負莎翁本人所託，也為後人留下珍貴而豐富的文化資源，其中不僅包括美妙動人的詞句，還有各種人物的性格塑造與著墨。

除了作品，莎士比亞本人也在生前受到讚揚。班・強生曾說他是個「正人君子，天性開放自由，想像力出奇，擁有大無畏的思想，言詞溫和，蘊含機智」。也有學者以勇敢、敏感、平衡、幽默和身心健康這五種特質來形容莎士比亞，並說他「將無私的愛奉為至上，認為罪惡的根源是恐懼，而非金錢。」

因為這些劇本刻畫入微，具有知性，有人認為不可能是未受過大學教育的莎士比亞所作，因而引發爭議。有人推測出真正的作者，其中較為人所知的有法蘭西斯・培根（Francis Bacon）和牛津的德維爾公爵（Edward de Vere of Oxford），後者形成了頗具影響力的牛津學派。儘管傳說繪聲繪影，各種假說和研究不斷，但大概沒有人會說莎士比亞是虛構人物。

左：姊姊瑪麗（Mary Lamb, 1764–1847）
右：弟弟查爾斯（Charles Lamb, 1775–1834）

作者簡介：蘭姆姊弟

姊姊瑪麗（Mary Lamb）生於 1764 年，弟弟查爾斯（Charles Lamb）於 1775 年也在倫敦呱呱落地。因為家境不夠寬裕，瑪麗沒有接受過完整的教育。她從小就做針線活，幫忙持家，照顧母親。查爾斯在學生時代結識了詩人柯立芝（Samuel Taylor Coleridge），兩人成為終生的朋友。查爾斯後來因家中經濟困難而輟學，1792 年轉而就職於東印度公司（East India House），這是他謀生的終身職業。

查爾斯在二十歲時一度精神崩潰，瑪麗則因為長年工作過量，在 1796 年突然精神病發，持刀攻擊父母，母親不幸傷重身亡。這件人倫悲劇發生後，瑪麗被判為精神異常，送往精神病院。查爾斯為此放棄自己原本期待的婚姻，以便全心照顧姊姊，使她免於在精神病院終老。

十九世紀的英國教育重視莎翁作品，一般的中產階級家庭也希望孩子早點接觸莎劇。1806 年，文學家兼編輯高德溫（William Godwin）邀請查爾斯協助「少年圖書館」的出版計畫，請他將莎翁的劇本改寫為適合兒童閱讀的故事。

查爾斯接受這項工作後就與瑪麗合作，他負責六齣悲劇，瑪麗負責十四齣喜劇並撰寫前言。瑪麗在後來曾描述說，他們兩人

蘭姆姊弟的《莎士比亞故事集》（*Tales from Shakespeare*）
1922 年版的卷首插畫

「就坐在同一張桌子上改寫，看起來就好像《仲夏夜之夢》裡的荷米雅與海蓮娜一樣。」就這樣，姊弟兩人合力完成了這一系列的莎士比亞故事。《莎士比亞故事集》在 1807 年出版後便大受好評，建立了查爾斯的文學聲譽。

查爾斯的寫作風格獨特，筆法樸實，主題豐富。他將自己的一生，包括童年時代、基督教會學校的生活、東印度公司的光陰、與瑪麗相伴的點點滴滴，以及自己的白日夢、鍾愛的書籍和友人等等，都融入在文章裡，作品充滿細膩情感和豐富的想像力。他的軟弱、怪異、魅力、幽默、口吃，在在都使讀者感到親切熟悉，而獨特的筆法與敘事方式，也使他成為英國出色的散文大師。

1823 年，查爾斯和瑪麗領養了一個孤兒愛瑪。兩年後，查爾斯自東印度公司退休，獲得豐厚的退休金。查爾斯的健康情形和瑪麗的精神狀況卻每況愈下。 1833 年，愛瑪嫁給出版商後，又只剩下姊弟兩人。 1834 年 7 月，由於幼年時代的好友柯立芝去世，查爾斯的精神一蹶不振，沉湎酒精。此年秋天，查爾斯在散步時不慎跌倒，傷及顏面，後來傷口竟惡化至不可收拾的地步，而於年底過世。

查爾斯善與人交，和許多文人都保持良好情誼，又因為他一生對姊姊的照顧不餘遺力，所以也廣受敬佩。查爾斯和瑪麗兩人都終生未婚，查爾斯曾在一篇伊利亞小品中，將他們的狀況形容為「雙重單身」（double singleness）。查爾斯去世後，瑪麗的心理狀態雖然漸趨惡化，但一直到十三年後才辭世。

A Midsummer Night's Dream

仲夏夜之夢

《仲夏夜之夢》導讀

《仲夏夜之夢》是莎劇中最常被搬演改編也是最受歡迎的喜劇之一，有不少人都還是透過《仲夏夜之夢》開始接觸到莎翁作品。近幾十年來，此劇因為含有夢的成分，因此受到不少心理分析大師的青睞。又因內容提及父親意圖掌握女兒、仙王想要控制仙后的橋段，因此也有人引用女性主義來探討此劇。

本劇敘述雅典城內的一對戀人荷米雅和萊桑德，荷米雅的父親反對他們在一起，他要求公爵下令，如果荷米雅不肯嫁給德米崔斯，就要判她死罪。於是這對戀人決定逃出雅典，而喜歡荷米雅的德米崔斯，以及迷戀德米崔斯的海蓮娜，也跟隨這對戀人逃進森林。

林子裡的仙王歐伯龍為幫助海蓮娜，就命令帕克趁德米崔斯睡著時，把神奇的情水滴在他的眼皮上，待他醒來，就會愛上睜眼後第一個看到的人。未料陰錯陽差，帕克搞錯對象，把情水滴在萊桑德的眼上，使萊桑德愛上海蓮娜。

歐伯龍得知後，趕緊把情水滴在德米崔斯的眼睛裡，讓他也愛上海蓮娜，然後再把解藥倒進萊桑德的眼睛裡解除魔法。荷米雅的父親發現荷米雅和德米崔斯各有意中人後，也就答應了兩人的婚事。最後，這兩對戀人就雙雙在同一天舉行婚禮。

真實與夢幻

整場戲就情節推演而言，可分三個部分：首先是一條地位崇高卻荒謬無比的律法；其次，劇中男女人物逃往林子後，精靈的介入使彼此愛戀的對象混淆，因而產生誤解與衝突；最後，一陣混亂之後，終於恢復理智和諧。本故事發生在仲夏夜晚，故事的主人翁們一度失去自我，事實上在西方文化中，有所謂的「仲夏瘋」（midsummer madness）和「月暈」（moonstruck），象徵著黎明之時，混亂才能回復秩序，疑惑衝突才會得到解決。

此劇兩兩對比的元素，如幾何圖形般對稱，故事發生於城市與森林、清醒與睡眠、真實與夢幻之間。底修斯掌管現實的雅典城，歐伯龍則是夢幻的森林之王，分別象徵理智和潛意識。

森林代表激情、焦慮、混亂、不受管束，隱藏著許多不可預測的因素，甚至有身分錯置的危機，彷彿是一場紛擾的夢境，時空與真實世界截然不同。雅典城代表社會機制和社會運作的秩序，足以化解所有的衝突。

鄉巴佬和帕克這兩個角色，正可以當作真實世界與夢幻世界的代表人物。庸俗也好，質樸也罷，許多評論家特別中意鄉巴佬這個角色，認為他腳踏實地，對仙后的地位和法力不為所動，只關心找到路回家、覓食、搔癢、睡覺。帕克則是抱持遊戲人間的態度，他捉弄村民，對自己找錯對象、滴錯情水不但不以為意，還覺得很有趣味，代表了對脫序狀態的偏好。

另一個對稱的安排是兩兩成雙的戀人，萊桑德和德米崔斯，荷米雅和海蓮娜，他們之間的角色互換，撲朔迷離。

原創性的劇情

本劇看似簡單，實則具有不凡的文學與戲劇價值。另外，在莎翁眾多的劇本當中，《仲夏夜之夢》也是少數極具原創性的劇本，不像其他大部分的劇本，取材其他作品而加以融合改編。

此劇約於 1595–1596 年間完成，雖然可能只是為一般大眾而寫的通俗劇，但也有部分學者認為是因應某節慶或某貴族婚禮而寫，所以充滿希望和歡娛氣氛。現代曆法的仲夏指的是六月二十四日，但劇中提及五月節慶，所以故事發生的時間可能在五月。在早期，只有夏秋冬三個季節，夏天包含春天，所以仲夏便落在五月初，但莎士比亞並沒有明白點出確切的時間背景。

莎士比亞在當時期似乎特別偏好「夢」，在同時期的作品《理查二世》和《羅密歐與茱麗葉》中，「夢」字的出現也特別頻繁，而「夢」在這三個劇本中出現的次數，就占了他所有劇作的三分之一。夢境光怪陸離，醒來之後，雖知其不可思議，卻不會令人無法接受，這就是夢的特質。潛意識藉由我們可感知的方式，在夢裡呈現出來。夢處理不同於理性的情緒，透露我們的真正想法、感覺、欲望或恐懼等等，揭露隱而不見的潛意識。夢也帶有預示作用，預示未來的可能變化。

據此，仲夏夜之「夢」屬於預示的夢，夢醒後，戀情圓滿成雙，好友重修舊好，死罪撤銷。但仲夏夜之「夢」又不是真正的夢，夢醒後之所以圓滿，乃是因為精靈從中介入，所以劇終

時，劇中人才會告訴觀眾讀者，如果本劇顯得似是而非、不合情理，那就當看戲是做夢，就把整齣戲看作是一場夢吧。

精靈與魔法

提到精靈，伊莉莎白時期的人們大都相信精靈的存在，鄉間尤其流傳精靈傳說。他們認為精靈和祖先凱爾特人（Celtic）同源，會騎馬打獵、跳舞歡宴，也能夠變身或是飛天隱形。精靈既對凡人慷慨贈與，也會懲戒凡人。他們處罰人類的方式常常是捏擰一把，或是用醜小孩來和人類的小孩調包。這些精靈一般都稱為帕克（puck，意指淘氣、喜歡惡作劇的小妖精）或者小妖魔（hobgoblin），他們多半喜歡在夜晚作怪，有些邪惡意味，有些大人會拿這些小妖怪來嚇唬不聽話的孩子。

此外，神話傳說中的仙王一般就叫做歐伯龍（Oberon），仙后則稱為戴安娜（Diana）、辛西亞（Cynthia）、妃比（Phoebe）或黑克悌（Hecate）等，而仙王的地位通常略遜於仙后。漸漸地，人們不再信仰精靈，但精靈仍成為通俗的娛樂文化中受人歡迎的主題，尤其是台上歌舞表演的主要角色。《仲夏夜之夢》對仙王、仙后和帕克的描述，大致與傳說吻合，這顯示莎士比亞熟悉民間傳說。他直接沿用各種傳說，唯獨仙后泰坦妮的名字取自歐維德的《變形記》。另外，帕克愛捉弄人，卻無惡意，這似乎也是莎翁的創舉。

本齣戲有許多場景特別適於劇場表現，例如夏夜森林、森林精靈、精靈魔法、好事多磨的兩對戀人，或是仙后和驢頭鄉巴佬的滑稽邂逅等等。事實上，這部戲的演出史可以說就是精靈的造型史。十九世紀起，精靈的演出常由數十位歌者或舞者集體表現，他們或為兒童，或為少年，或為成人。此時，甚至也出現了東方造型的精靈。

此劇歷久不衰，深受喜愛。其一般的製作和演出，傾向以芭蕾劇或歌劇呈現，其中最著名的舞台演出是英國導演彼得・布魯克（Peter Brook）於 1970 年的作品，近年來則有羅伯・樂帕許（Robert Lepage）為英國國家劇院（National Theatre）執導的版本，有興趣的讀者可參考葛瑞飛茲（Trevor R. Griffiths）所編纂的《仲夏夜之夢》演出紀錄，而喜好電影的讀者，也可能看過多部電影版的《仲夏夜之夢》。

《仲夏夜之夢》人物表

Oberon	歐伯龍	精靈國的仙王
Titania	泰坦妮	精靈國的仙后
Puck	帕克	精靈，歐伯龍的差使
Hermia	荷米雅	因父親將她許配給德米崔斯，準備和情人萊桑德私奔
Lysander	萊桑德	和荷米雅是一對戀人
Helena	海蓮娜	荷米雅的好友，喜歡德米崔斯
Demetrius	德米崔斯	一位貴族青年

A Midsummer Night's Dream

🎧 **1** There was a law in the city of Athens which gave to its citizens the power of compelling[1] their daughters to marry whomsoever they pleased; for upon a daughter's refusing to marry the man her father had chosen to be her husband, the father was empowered by this law to cause her to be put to death; but as fathers do not often desire the death of their own daughters, even though they do happen to prove a little refractory[2], this law was seldom or never put in execution[3], though perhaps the young ladies of that city were not unfrequently threatened by their parents with the terrors of it.

There was one instance, however, of an old man, whose name was Egeus, who actually did come before Theseus (at that time the reigning duke of Athens), to complain that his daughter Hermia, whom he had commanded to marry Demetrius, a young man of a noble Athenian family, refused to obey him, because she loved another young Athenian, named Lysander. Egeus demanded justice of Theseus, and desired that this cruel law might be put in force against his daughter.

Hermia pleaded[4] in excuse for her disobedience, that Demetrius had formerly professed love for her dear friend Helena, and that Helena loved Demetrius to distraction[5]; but this honorable reason, which Hermia gave for not obeying her father's command, moved not the stern Egeus.

Theseus, though a great and merciful prince, had no power to alter the laws of his country; therefore he could only give Hermia four days to consider of it and at the end of that time, if she still refused to marry Demetrius, she was to be put to death.

1 compel [kəm'pel] (v.) 強迫
2 refractory [rɪ'fræktəri] (a.) 執拗的
3 execution [ˌeksɪ'kjuːʃən] (n.) 執行；實行
4 plead [pliːd] (v.) 抗辯
5 distraction [dɪ'strækʃən] (n.) 發狂

BYAM·SHAW

BVT·I·WILL·WED·THEE·IN
ANOTHER·KEY ACT·I·SCENE·I·

When Hermia was dismissed from the presence of the duke, she went to her lover Lysander, and told him the peril[6] she was in, and that she must either give him up and marry Demetrius, or lose her life in four days.

Lysander was in great affliction[7] at hearing these evil tidings[8]; but recollecting that he had an aunt who lived at some distance from Athens, and that at the place where she lived the cruel law could not be put in force against Hermia (this law not extending beyond the boundaries of the city), he proposed to Hermia that she should steal out of her father's house that night, and go with him to his aunt's house, where he would marry her.

"I will meet you," said Lysander, "in the wood a few miles without the city; in that delightful wood where we have so often walked with Helena in the pleasant month of May."

6 peril ['perəl] (n.) 危險
7 affliction [ə'flɪkʃən] (n.) 痛苦；苦難
8 tidings ['taɪdɪŋz] (n.) 〔古代用法〕〔複數形〕消息；音信

To this proposal Hermia joyfully agreed; and she told no one of her intended flight[9] but her friend Helena. Helena (as maidens will do foolish things for love) very ungenerously resolved[10] to go and tell this to Demetrius, though she could hope no benefit from betraying her friend's secret, but the poor pleasure of following her faithless lover to the wood; for she well knew that Demetrius would go thither[11] in pursuit of Hermia.

The wood in which Lysander and Hermia proposed to meet, was the favorite haunt of those little beings known by the name of *Fairies*.

Oberon the king, and Titania the queen of the Fairies, with all their tiny train[12] of followers, in this wood held their midnight revels[13].

---

9 flight [flaɪt] (n.) 逃亡；逃走
10 resolve [rɪˈzɑːlv] (v.) 決定；決心
11 thither [ˈθɪðər] (adv.) 〔舊時用法〕到彼處
12 train [treɪn] (n.) 成縱隊行進的若干人、車輛等隊伍
13 revel [ˈrɛvəl] (n.) 作樂；狂歡享樂

🎧 4 Between this little king and queen of sprites there happened, at this time, a sad disagreement; they never met by moonlight in the shady walks of this pleasant wood, but they were quarreling, till all their fairy elves[14] would creep[15] into acorn-cups and hide themselves for fear.

The cause of this unhappy disagreement was Titania's refusing to give Oberon a little changeling[16] boy, whose mother had been Titania's friend; and upon her death the fairy queen stole the child from its nurse, and brought him up in the woods.

The night on which the lovers were to meet in this wood, as Titania was walking with some of her maids of honor, she met Oberon attended by his train of fairy courtiers[17].

"I'll met by moonlight, proud Titania," said the fairy king.

The queen replied, "What, jealous Oberon, is it you? Fairies, skip hence; I have forsworn[18] his company."

14 elf [ɛlf] (n.) 小精靈（複數形作 elves）

15 creep [kriːp] (v.) 爬行；匍匐

16 changeling [ˈtʃeɪndʒlɪŋ] (n.) 調包小孩（傳說被調包後的醜小孩）

17 courtier [ˈkɔːrtɪr] (n.) 朝臣

18 forswear [fɔrˈswɛr] (v.) 放棄；戒絕

"Tarry[19], rash fairy," said Oberon; "am not I thy lord? Why does Titania cross her Oberon? Give me your little changeling boy to be my page[20]."

"Set your heart at rest," answered the queen; "your whole fairy kingdom buys not the boy of me." She then left her lord in great anger.

"Well, go your way," said Oberon: "before the morning dawns I will torment[21] you for this injury."

Oberon then sent for Puck, his chief favorite and privy counselor. Puck (or as he was sometimes called, Robin Good-fellow) was a shrewd[22] and knavish[23] sprite, that used to play comical pranks in the neighboring villages; sometimes getting into the dairies and skimming the milk, sometimes plunging[24] his light and airy form into the butter-churn[25], and while he was dancing his fantastic shape in the churn, in vain the dairy-maid would labor to change her cream into butter: nor had the village swains[26] any better success; whenever Puck chose to play his freaks[27] in the brewing copper[28], the ale was sure to be spoiled.

19 tarry [ˈtæri] (v.) 逗留;停留
20 page [peɪdʒ] (n.) 僮僕
21 torment [ˈtɔːrment] (v.) 折磨
22 shrewd [ʃruːd] (a.) 狡獪的
23 knavish [ˈneɪvɪʃ] (a.) 無賴的
24 plunge [plʌndʒ] (v.) 投入
25 butter-churn [ˈbʌtərˌtʃɜːrn] (n.) 攪乳器
26 swain [sweɪn] (n.)〔詩的用法〕〔古代用法〕年輕的鄉下人
27 freak [friːk] (n.) 怪誕的思想、行動或事件
28 copper [ˈkɑːpər] (n.) 金屬鍋

butter-churn

When a few good neighbors were met to drink some comfortable ale together, Puck would jump into the bowl of ale in the likeness of a roasted crab, and when some old goody[29] was going to drink he would bob[30] against her lips, and spill the ale over her withered chin; and presently after, when the same old dame was gravely seating herself to tell her neighbors a sad and melancholy story, Puck would slip her three-legged stool from under her, and down toppled[31] the poor old woman, and then the old gossips would hold their sides[32] and laugh at her, and swear they never wasted a merrier hour.

"Come hither, Puck," said Oberon to this little merry wanderer of the night; "fetch me the flower which maids call Love in Idleness; the juice of that little purple flower laid on the eyelids of those who sleep, will make them, when they awake, dote[33] on the first thing they see. Some of the juice of that flower I will drop on the eyelids of my Titania when she is asleep; and the first thing she looks upon when she opens her eyes she will fall in love with, even though it be a lion or a bear, a meddling[34] monkey,

Love in Idleness

or a busy ape; and before I will take this charm from off her sight, which I can do with another charm I know of, I will make her give me that boy to be my page."

Puck, who loved mischief to his heart, was highly diverted with this intended frolic[35] of his master, and ran to seek the flower; and while Oberon was waiting the return of Puck, he observed Demetrius and Helena enter the wood: he overheard Demetrius reproaching Helena for following him, and after many unkind words on his part, and gentle expostulations[36] from Helena, reminding him of his former love and professions of true faith to her, he left her (as he said) to the mercy of the wild beasts, and she ran after him as swiftly as she could.

29 goody ['gʊdi] (n.) 低下階層的老婦
30 bob [bɑːb] (v.) 上下移動
31 topple ['tɑːpəl] (v.) 搖搖欲墜
32 hold one's sides 捧腹大笑
33 dote [doʊt] (v.) 溺愛；寵
34 meddling ['medlɪŋ] (a.) 妨礙的；干擾的
35 frolic ['frɑːlɪk] (n.) 嬉戲；作樂
36 expostulation [ɪkˌspɑːstʃʊ'leɪʃən] (n.) 告誡；勸誡

The fairy king, who was always friendly to true lovers, felt great compassion for Helena; and perhaps, as Lysander said they used to walk by moonlight in this pleasant wood, Oberon might have seen Helena in those happy times when she was beloved by Demetrius.

However that might be, when Puck returned with the little purple flower, Oberon said to his favorite, "Take a part of this flower; there has been a sweet Athenian lady here, who is in love with a disdainful[37] youth; if you find him sleeping, drop some of the love-juice in his eyes, but contrive[38] to do it when she is near him, that the first thing he sees when he awakes may be this despised[39] lady. You will know the man by the Athenian garments which he wears."

Puck promised to manage this matter very dexterously[40]: and then Oberon went, unperceived by Titania, to her bower[41], where she was preparing to go to rest. Her fairy bower was a bank, where grew wild thyme[42], cowslips[43], and sweet violets, under a canopy of woodbine, musk-roses, and eglantine[44]. There Titania always slept some part of the night; her coverlet the enameled[45] skin of a snake, which, though a small mantle[46], was wide enough to wrap a fairy in.

37 disdainful [dɪsˈdeɪnfəl] (a.) 輕蔑的
38 contrive [kənˈtraɪv] (v.) 想辦法；動腦筋
39 despised [dɪˈspaɪzd] (a.) 受人輕視的
40 dexterously [ˈdekstərəsli] (adv.) 雙手靈巧地
41 bower [ˈbaʊər] (n.) 〔文學用法〕閨房
42 thyme [taɪm] (n.) 百里香
43 cowslip [ˈkaʊslɪp] (n.) 野櫻草
44 eglantine [ˈeɡləntaɪn] (n.) 野薔薇
45 enameled [ɪˈnæməld] (a.) 瓷釉的
46 mantle [ˈmæntl] (n.) 斗篷；〔比喻用法〕覆蓋物

cowslip

He found Titania giving orders to her fairies, how they were to employ themselves while she slept. "Some of you," said her majesty, "must kill cankers[47] in the musk-rose buds, and some wage war with the bats for their leathern wings, to make my small elves coats; and some of you keep watch that the clamorous[48] owl, that nightly hoots[49], come not near me: but first sing me to sleep."

Then they began to sing this song—

> *You spotted snakes with double tongue,*
> *Thorny hedgehogs[50], be not seen;*
> *Newts[51] and blindworms, do no wrong,*
> *Come not near our Fairy Queen.*
> *Philomel[52], with melody,*
> *Sing in our sweet lullaby,*
> *Lulla, lulla, lullaby; lulla, lulla, lullaby;*
> *Never harm, nor spell, nor charm,*
> *Come our lovely lady nigh[53];*
> *So good night with lullaby.*

47 canker ['kæŋkər] (n.) 動、植物的潰瘍病

48 clamorous ['klæmərəs] (a.) 吵鬧的；叫喊的

49 hoot [huːt] (n.) 梟叫聲 (v.) 作貓頭鷹叫聲

50 hedgehog ['hedʒɑːg] (n.) 刺蝟

51 newt [njuːt] (n.) 蠑螈

52 philomel ['fɪləmel] (n.) 夜鶯

53 nigh [naɪ] (adv.) (prep.) 〔古代用法〕〔詩的用法〕靠近

When the fairies had sung their queen asleep with this pretty lullaby, they left her to perform the important services she had enjoined them. Oberon then softly drew near his Titania, and dropped some of the love-juice on her eyelids, saying—

> *What thou seest when them dost[54] wake,*
> *Do it for thy true-love take.*

But to return to Hermia, who made her escape out of her father's house that night, to avoid the death she was doomed to for refusing to marry Demetrius. When she entered the wood, she found her dear Lysander waiting for her, to conduct her to his aunt's house; but before they had passed half through the wood, Hermia was so much fatigued, that Lysander, who was very careful of this dear lady, who had proved her affection for him even by hazarding[55] her life for his sake, persuaded her to rest till morning on a bank of soft moss, and lying down himself on the ground at some little distance, they soon fell fast asleep.

---

54 dost [dʌst] (v.) 〔古代用法〕do 的第二人稱單數，與 thou 連用
55 hazard [ˈhæzərd] (v.) 使遭受危險

Here they were found by Puck, who, seeing a handsome young man asleep, and perceiving that his clothes were made in the Athenian fashion, and that a pretty lady was sleeping near him, concluded that this must be the Athenian maid and her disdainful lover whom Oberon had sent him to seek; and he naturally enough conjectured[56] that, as they were alone together, she must be the first thing he would see when he awoke; so, without more ado[57], he proceeded to pour some of the juice of the little purple flower into his eyes.

But it so fell out, that Helena came that way, and, instead of Hermia, was the first object Lysander beheld when he opened his eyes; and strange to relate, so powerful was the love-charm, all his love for Hermia vanished away, and Lysander fell in love with Helena.

Had he first seen Hermia when he awoke, the blunder Puck committed would have been of no consequence, for he could not love that faithful lady too well.

But for poor Lysander to be forced by a fairy love-charm, to forget his own true Hermia, and to run after another lady, and leave Hermia asleep quite alone in a wood at midnight, was a sad chance indeed.

56 conjecture [kənˈdʒektʃər] (v.) 猜測；推想
57 ado [əˈduː] (n.) 〔古代用法〕無謂的紛擾

🎧 11 Thus this misfortune happened. Helena, as has been before related, endeavored to keep pace with Demetrius when he ran away so rudely from her; but she could not continue this unequal race long, men being always better runners in a long race than ladies. Helena soon lost sight of Demetrius; and as she was wandering about, dejected[58] and forlorn[59], she arrived at the place where Lysander was sleeping.

"Ah!" said she, "this is Lysander lying on the ground: is he dead or asleep?" Then, gently touching him, she said, "Good sir, if you are alive, awake."

Upon this Lysander opened his eyes, and (the love-charm beginning to work) immediately addressed her in terms of extravagant[60] love and admiration; telling her she as much excelled Hermia in beauty as a dove does a raven, and that he would run through fire for her sweet sake; and many more such lover-like speeches.

---

58 dejected [dɪ'dʒektɪd] (a.) 悲傷的；沮喪的
59 forlorn [fər'lɔːrn] (a.) 〔詩的用法〕〔文學用法〕不幸的；孤零的
60 extravagant [ɪk'strævəgənt] (a.) （指思想、言論、行為）過分的

Helena, knowing Lysander was her friend Hermia's lover, and that he was solemnly engaged to marry her, was in the utmost rage when she heard herself addressed in this manner; for she thought (as well she might) that Lysander was making a jest[61] of her.

"Oh!" said she, "why was I born to be mocked and scorned[62] by every one? Is it not enough, is it not enough, young man, that I can never get a sweet look or a kind word from Demetrius; but you, sir, must pretend in this disdainful manner to court me? I thought, Lysander, you were a lord of more true gentleness."

Saying these words in great anger, she ran away; and Lysander followed her, quite forgetful of his own Hermia, who was still asleep.

When Hermia awoke, she was in a sad fright[63] at finding herself alone. She wandered about the wood, not knowing what was become of Lysander, or which way to go to seek for him.

In the meantime Demetrius not being able to find Hermia and his rival Lysander, and fatigued with his fruitless search, was observed by Oberon fast asleep. Oberon had learnt by some questions he had asked of Puck, that he had applied the love-charm to the wrong person's eyes; and now having found the person first intended, he touched the eyelids of the sleeping Demetrius with the love-juice, and he instantly awoke; and the first thing he saw being Helena, he, as Lysander had done before, began to address love-speeches to her; and just as that moment Lysander, followed by Hermia (for through Puck's unlucky mistake it was now become Hermia's turn to run after her lover), made his appearance; and then Lysander and Demetrius, both speaking together, made love to Helena, they being each one under the influence of the same potent[64] charm.

61 jest [dʒest] (n.) 笑柄
62 scorn [skɔːrn] (v.) 輕蔑
63 fright [fraɪt] (n.) 驚駭
64 potent ['poutənt] (a.) （非用於人或機器）有力的；有效的

The astonished Helena thought that Demetrius, Lysander, and her once dear friend Hermia, were all in a plot together to make a jest of her.

Hermia was as much surprised as Helena: she knew not why Lysander and Demetrius, who both before loved her, were now become the lovers of Helena; and to Hermia the matter seemed to be no jest.

The ladies, who before had always been the dearest of friends, now fell to high words together.

"Unkind Hermia," said Helena, "it is you who have set Lysander to vex[65] me with mock praises; and your other lover Demetrius, who used almost to spurn[66] me with his foot, have you not bid him call me Goddess, Nymph, rare, precious, and celestial[67]? He would not speak thus to me, whom he hates, if you did not set him on to make a jest of me. Unkind Hermia, to join with men in scorning your poor friend. Have you forgot our school-day friendship? How often, Hermia, have we two, sitting on one cushion, both singing one song, with our needles working the same flower, both on the same sampler wrought[68]; growing up together in fashion of a double cherry, scarcely seeming parted!

Hermia, it is not friendly in you, it is not maidenly to join with men in scorning your poor friend."

"I am amazed at your passionate words," said Hermia: "I scorn you not; it seems you scorn me."

"Ay, do," returned Helena, "persevere[69], counterfeit[70] serious looks, and make mouths at me when I turn my back; then wink at each other, and hold the sweet jest up. If you had any pity, grace, or manners, you would not use me thus."

While Helena and Hermia were speaking these angry words to each other, Demetrius and Lysander left them, to fight together in the wood for the love of Helena.

When they found the gentlemen had left them, they departed, and once more wandered weary in the wood in search of their lovers.

---

65 vex [veks] (v.) 使惱怒；苦惱
66 spurn [spɜːrn] (v.) 輕蔑地拒絕
67 celestial [sɪˈlestʃəl] (a.) 極佳的；天國的；神聖的
68 wrought [rɑːt] (a.) 〔舊的用法〕製成的（work 的過去式）
69 persevere [ˌpɜːrsɪˈvɪr] (v.) 堅忍；堅持
70 counterfeit [ˈkaʊntərfɪt] (v.) 偽造；假裝

Oberon and Puck

As soon as they were gone, the fairy king, who with little Puck had been listening to their quarrels, said to him, "This is your negligence, Puck; or did you do this wilfully?"

"Believe me, king of shadows," answered Puck, "it was a mistake; did not you tell me I should know the man by his Athenian garments? However, I am not sorry this has happened, for I think their jangling[71] makes excellent sport."

"You heard," said Oberon, "that Demetrius and Lysander are gone to seek a convenient place to fight in. I command you to overhang the night with a thick fog, and lead these quarrelsome lovers so astray in the dark, that they shall not be able to find each other. Counterfeit each of their voices to the other, and with bitter taunts[72] provoke them to follow you, while they think it is their rival's tongue they hear. See you do this, till they are so weary they can go no farther; and when you find they are asleep, drop the juice of this other flower into Lysander's eyes, and when he awakes he will forget his new love for Helena, and return to his old passion for Hermia; and then the two fair ladies may each one be happy with the man she loves, and they will think all that has passed a vexatious dream. About this quickly, Puck, and I will go and see what sweet love my Titania has found."

71 jangling [ˈdʒæŋɡəlɪŋ] (n.) 喧鬧的爭論
72 taunt [tɔːnt] (n.) 辱罵；嘲弄

Titania was still sleeping, and Oberon seeing a clown near her, who had lost his way in the wood, and was likewise asleep: "This fellow," said he, "shall be my Titania's true love;" and clapping[73] an ass's head over the clown's, it seemed to fit him as well as if it had grown upon his own shoulders.

Though Oberon fixed the ass's head on very gently, it awakened him, and rising up, unconscious of what Oberon had done to him, he went towards the bower where the fairy queen slept.

"Ah! what angel is that I see?" said Titania, opening her eyes, and the juice of the little purple flower beginning to take effect: "are you as wise as you are beautiful?"

"Why, mistress," said the foolish clown, "if I have wit enough to find the way out of this wood, I have enough to serve my turn."

"Out of the wood do not desire to go," said the enamored[74] queen. "I am a spirit of no common rate. I love you. Go with me, and I will give you fairies to attend upon you."

---

73 clap [klæp] (v.) 急速放置
74 enamored [ɪˈnæmərd] (a.) 痴心的

She then called four of her fairies: their names were, Pease-blossom, Cobweb, Moth, and Mustard-seed.

"Attend," said the queen, "upon this sweet gentleman; hop in his walks, and gambol[75] in his sight; feed him with grapes and apricots, and steal for him the honey-bags from the bees. Come, sit with me," said she to the clown, "and let me play with your amiable hairy cheeks, my beautiful ass! and kiss your fair large ears, my gentle joy!"

"Where is Pease-blossom?" said the ass-headed clown, not much regarding the fairy queen's courtship, but very proud of his new attendants.

"Here, sir," said little Pease-blossom.

"Scratch my head," said the clown. "Where is Cobweb?"

"Here, sir," said Cobweb.

75 gambol ['gæmbəl] (v.) 雀躍；嬉戲

"Good Mr. Cobweb," said the foolish clown, "kill me the red humblebee on the top of that thistle[76] yonder; and, good Mr. Cobweb, bring me the honey-bag. Do not fret[77] yourself too much in the action, Mr. Cobweb, and take care the honey-bag break not; I should be sorry to have you overflown with a honey-bag. Where is Mustard-seed?"

"Here, sir," said Mustard-seed: "what is your will?"

"Nothing," said the clown, "good Mr. Mustard-seed, but to help Mr. Pease-blossom to scratch; I must go to a barber's, Mr. Mustard-seed, for methinks I am marvelous hairy about the face."

"My sweet love," said the queen, "what will you have to eat? I have a venturous fairy shall seek the squirrel's hoard[78], and fetch you some new nuts."

"I had rather have a handful of dried pease[79]," said the clown, who with his ass's head had got an ass's appetite. "But, I pray, let none of your people disturb me, for I have a mind to sleep."

76 thistle [θɪsl] (n.)〔植物〕薊
77 fret [frɛt] (v.) 煩惱;煩躁
78 hoard [hɔːrd] (n.) 節省下來妥善保存的食物
79 pease [piːz] (n.)〔已廢棄的用法〕豌豆

thistle

58

"Sleep, then," said the queen, "and I will wind you in my arms. O how I love you! how I dote upon you!"

When the fairy king saw the clown sleeping in the arms of his queen, he advanced within her sight, and reproached her with having lavished[80] her favors upon an ass.

This she could not deny, as the clown was then sleeping within her arms, with his ass's head crowned by her with flowers.

When Oberon had teased her for some time, he again demanded the changeling boy; which she, ashamed of being discovered by her lord with her new favorite, did not dare to refuse him.

Oberon, having thus obtained the little boy he had so long wished for to be his page, took pity on the disgraceful situation into which, by his merry contrivance, he had brought his Titania, and threw some of the juice of the other flower into her eyes; and the fairy queen immediately recovered her senses, and wondered at her late dotage, saying how she now loathed[81] the sight of the strange monster.

80　lavish ['lævɪʃ] (v.) 慷慨贈與
81　loathe [louð] (v.) 厭惡

Oberon likewise took the ass's head from off the clown, and left him to finish his nap with his own fool's head upon his shoulders.

Oberon and his Titania being now perfectly reconciled[82], he related to her the history of the lovers, and their midnight quarrels; and she agreed to go with him and see the end of their adventures.

The fairy king and queen found the lovers and their fair ladies, at no great distance from each other, sleeping on a grass-plot; for Puck, to make amends[83] for his former mistake, had contrived with the utmost diligence[84] to bring them all to the same spot, unknown to each other; and he had carefully removed the charm from off the eyes of Lysander with the antidote[85] the fairy king gave to him.

Hermia first awoke, and finding her lost Lysander asleep so near her, was looking at him and wondering at his strange inconstancy. Lysander presently opening his eyes, and seeing his dear Hermia, recovered his reason which the fairy charm had before clouded, and with his reason, his love for Hermia; and they began to talk over the adventures of the night, doubting if these things had really happened, or if they had both been dreaming the same bewildering[86] dream.

82 reconcile [ˈrekənsaɪl] (v.) 爭吵後和好；和解

83 amends [əˈmendz] (n.) 〔用複數形〕補償

84 diligence [ˈdɪlədʒəns] (n.) 勤勉

85 antidote [ˈæntɪdoʊt] (n.) 解藥；抗毒劑

86 bewildering [bɪˈwɪldərɪŋ] (a.) 迷惑的；手足無措的

Helena and Demetrius were by this time awake; and a sweet sleep having quieted Helena's disturbed and angry spirits, she listened with delight to the professions of love which Demetrius still made to her, and which, to her surprise as well as pleasure, she began to perceive were sincere.

These fair night-wandering ladies, now no longer rivals, became once more true friends; all the unkind words which had passed were forgiven, and they calmly consulted together what was best to be done in their present situation. It was soon agreed that, as Demetrius had given up his pretensions[87] to Hermia, he should endeavor to prevail upon her father to revoke[88] the cruel sentence of death which had been passed against her. Demetrius was preparing to return to Athens for this friendly purpose, when they were surprised with the sight of Egeus, Hermia's father, who came to the wood in pursuit of his runaway daughter.

When Egeus understood that Demetrius would not now marry his daughter, he no longer opposed her marriage with Lysander, but gave his consent that they should be wedded on the fourth day from that time, being the same day on which Hermia had been condemned[89] to lose her life; and on that same day Helena joyfully agreed to marry her beloved and now faithful Demetrius.

The fairy king and queen, who were invisible spectators of this reconciliation, and now saw the happy ending of the lovers' history, brought about through the good offices[90] of Oberon, received so much pleasure, that these kind spirits resolved to celebrate the approaching nuptials[91] with sports and revels throughout their fairy kingdom.

And now, if any are offended with this story of fairies and their pranks, as judging it incredible and strange, they have only to think that they have been asleep and dreaming, and that all these adventures were visions which they saw in their sleep; and I hope none of my readers will be so unreasonable as to be offended with a pretty harmless Midsummer Night's Dream.

---

87 pretensions [prɪˈtenʃənz] (n.)〔常用複數形〕要求；權利；主張
88 revoke [rɪˈvouk] (v.) 撤銷；取消
89 condemn [kənˈdem] (v.) 判罪；處刑
90 offices [ˈɔːfɪsəz] (n.)〔複數形〕殷勤；服務
91 nuptials [ˈnʌpʃəlz] (n.)〔複數形〕婚禮

《仲夏夜之夢》名句選

Lysander	The course of true love never did run smooth;
	But, either it was different in blood
Hermia	O cross! too high to be enthrall'd to low.
Lysander	Or else misgraffed in respect of years
Hermia	O spite! too old to be engag'd to young.
Lysander	Or else it stood upon the choice of friends,
Hermia	O hell! to choose love by another's eye.
	(I, i, 134–40)

萊桑德	真愛之路永崎嶇；
	若非血統有差異—
荷米雅	不幸啊，身分懸殊難屈就！
萊桑德	便是年齡難以嫁接—
荷米雅	可惜啊，老少如何能婚配！
萊桑德	或聽憑友人之選擇—
荷米雅	倒楣啊，得憑外人眼光擇愛人！
	（第一幕，第一景，134–40行）

Puck Captain of our fairy band,
    Helena is here at hand,
    And the youth, mistook by me,
    Pleading for a lover's fee.
    Shall we their fond pageant see?
    Lord, what fools these mortals be!
    (III, ii, 110–15)

帕克 呈報仙界之首腦，
   已經帶來海蓮娜，
   身後隨來少年郎，
   苦苦哀求她瞥憐。
   瞧那癡戀的模樣，
   愚蠢凡人無法想！

   （第三幕，第二景，110–15 行）

The Merchant of Venice

威尼斯商人

《威尼斯商人》導讀

故事的來源

《威尼斯商人》又名《威尼斯的猶太人》（*The Jew of Venice*）。這齣戲劇於 1598 年首演，可能是莎士比亞在 1596–97 年間寫成的，主要情節由兩個常見的故事改編而成：

- 巴薩紐和波兒榭的故事：從一本名為 Il Pecorone（意指「大綿羊」或「笨蛋」）的義大利故事集之中獲得靈感。
- 賽拉客向安東尼索求一磅肉來當作賠償的故事：有多個來源，其中之一是 1596 年出版的《雄辯家》（*The Orator*）英譯本，作者為希爾維（Alexander Silvayn）。

猶太人取基督徒的肉並在逾越節（Passover）食用的說法，在中古時代早期就已流傳。基督徒相信猶太人曾加害耶穌基督，在伊莉莎白時期的劇場舞台上，賽拉客總是留著紅鬍鬚，長著鷹鉤鼻，模樣十足邪惡。莎翁當時代的人普遍認為：除非猶太人放棄其異教信仰和行為，否則基督徒很難原諒或接納他們。

文藝復興時期的歐洲人一提起猶太人，就聯想到放高利貸。在當時，放高利貸是普遍的生財之道，只是一般人在情緒上仍對其反感。他們認為放高利貸是道德上的罪行，這種獲利手段和經商不一樣，不需才智本錢，就可以賺取暴利，有時甚至近乎違法，而放高利貸的人的普遍形象則是腐敗、貪婪、吝嗇。

早於莎翁三百年的英王愛德華一世（Edward I, 在位其間為1272–1307 年）就曾下令將猶太人逐出英國，但在伊莉莎白時期，仍有部分猶太人居住在倫敦，只是他們礙於民風政令，必須隱瞞自己的身分及宗教信仰。

1589 年，英國劇作家馬婁（Christopher Marlowe）所寫的《馬爾他的猶太人》（*The Jew of Malta*）演出後，可能對莎士比亞造成了影響。馬婁所描寫的猶太人白若巴（Barabas）是個不折不扣的惡棍，為求目的不擇手段。劇中，白若巴沒有敵手，只有戲外的觀眾能譴責他，與莎士比亞所描寫的賽拉客有所不同。

猶太人角色

莎翁的賽拉客這一角色塑造得完整而真實。他頭腦精明，行事謹慎，口才流利，以放高利貸大發橫財，讓基督徒有憎恨他的理由。其中的衝突不只有種族和財務問題，也象徵了兩種全然不同的宗教、生活和價值觀。賽拉客過著節制吝嗇的生活，輕蔑基督徒生活的奢華浪費。事實上，在當時就常見威尼斯商人穿著華麗，宛如王室貴族。

另外，對賽拉客而言，善人的定義是經濟狀況足以維生，其他的道德或抽象的價值觀則毫無意義。劇中的基督徒與賽拉客代表完全不同的兩種人物，例如，巴薩紐因生活奢侈，造成阮囊羞澀，為了攀上一門闊親事，只得向好友借錢，好友則為其赴湯蹈火在所不惜，而賽拉客卻對金錢以外的東西都無動於衷。

波兒榭的角色

波兒榭所居住的背芒特（Belmont）在本劇中象徵一個不尋常的地點，這個地名的意思是「美麗的山丘」。當地平靜和諧，和擁擠紛亂、斤斤計較的威尼斯形成強烈對比。

波兒榭的住所象徵井然有序、物質生活不乏，而波兒榭本人更是具有理想的基督徒形象。她慷慨奉獻，洞察力敏銳，具有活力，反應靈敏。賽拉客僅依借據所載，不容變更。她以其人之道還治其人之身，致使賽拉客依約不得讓安東尼留下半滴血。這種破解的手法在當時廣為盛傳，也因此，莎翁主要要呈現的並不是令人激賞的機智，而是要表現波兒榭戰勝了邪惡。

除此之外，《威尼斯商人》也對愛情和友情多所著墨。曾有人試圖以同性戀來詮釋安東尼與巴薩紐之間的情誼，因為兩人都曾表示對方的性命勝於自己。儘管有這種指涉，但眾人最後返回背芒特的那一幕，似乎又暗示愛情更勝友情一籌。

波兒榭是本劇的女性靈魂人物，和賽拉客特別互相襯托。在故事中，基督徒對於批評持開放態度，猶太人則嚴守自己的行為準則。伊莉莎白時期，波兒榭較常成為此劇的核心人物。到了十九世紀，賽拉客卻時常躍昇為主角，使其他角色黯然失色，

甚至連最後在背芒特的逗趣一幕都被刪掉。評論家史鐸爾（E. E. Stoll）表示，伊莉莎白時期的民眾對吝嗇、放高利貸的猶太人存有根深柢固的偏見，故不足以成為本劇的中心人物。不過，賽拉客仍大受劇場演員的歡迎。

舞台上的搬演

舞台上詮釋賽拉客的方式有多種。他時而代表魔鬼的化身，時而成為喜劇裡的惡棍，偶爾也會展現受到曲解與委屈的可憐形象，引起觀眾的同情，蒙上了一層悲劇色彩。這種訴諸情感的詮釋手法由 1814 年英國演員愛德蒙・金（Edmund Kean）首創，其後也影響了勞倫斯・奧利佛（Laurence Olivier）對這個角色的詮釋。

現代的劇場則傾向於將賽拉客塑造成一名受害人。他因周遭人士對宗教抱持偏執頑固的立場而被誤解。這尤其表現在他自辯的那一段話上：難道因為宗教信仰不同，他就應該受到他人的道德倫理準則所批判嗎？莎士比亞以這段話呈現出賽拉客的人性。

二十世紀以後，《威尼斯商人》因對猶太人的偏見而引發不少種族議題，特別是二次世界大戰之後，此劇已轉為問題劇，多數人不再以輕鬆的眼光看待這個故事，原來的喜劇成分也就消失無蹤了。

《威尼斯商人》人物表

Shylock	賽拉客	一位放高利貸的猶太人
Antonio	安東尼	一位年輕的威尼斯商人
Bassanio	巴薩紐	安東尼的好友
Portia	波兒榭	巴薩紐的未婚妻
Gratiano	葛提諾	巴薩紐的友人
Nerissa	涅芮莎	波兒榭的貼身侍女

The Merchant of Venice

Shylock, the Jew, lived at Venice. He was a usurer[1], who had amassed[2] an immense fortune by lending money at great interest to Christian merchants. Shylock, being a hard-hearted man, exacted the payment of the money he lent with such severity[3] that he was much disliked by all good men, and particularly by Antonio, a young merchant of Venice; and Shylock as much hated Antonio, because he used to lend money to people in distress, and would never take any interest for the money he lent; therefore there was great enmity[4] between this covetous[5] Jew and the generous merchant Antonio. Whenever Antonio met Shylock on the Rialto[6] (or Exchange), he used to reproach[7] him with his usuries and hard dealings, which the Jew would bear with seeming patience, while he secretly meditated revenge.

1 usurer ['juːʒərər] (n.) 放高利貸者
2 amass [ə'mæs] (v.) 積聚（財富）
3 severity [sɪ'verɪti] (n.) 嚴厲

Shylock, Bassanio and Antonio

4 enmity ['enmɪti] (n.) 仇恨
5 covetous ['kʌvɪtəs] (a.) 貪圖的
6 Rialto [rɪ'ælto] (n.) 交易場所
7 reproach [rɪ'proutʃ] (v.) 斥責

22 Antonio was the kindest man that lived, the best conditioned, and had the most unwearied spirit in doing courtesies; indeed, he was one in whom the ancient Roman honor more appeared than in any that drew breath in Italy. He was greatly beloved by all his fellow-citizens; but the friend who was nearest and dearest to his heart was Bassanio, a noble Venetian, who, having but a small patrimony[8], had nearly exhausted his little fortune by living in too expensive a manner for his slender means, as young men of high rank with small fortunes are too apt to do. Whenever Bassanio wanted money, Antonio assisted him; and it seemed as if they had but one heart and one purse between them.

One day Bassanio came to Antonio, and told him that he wished to repair his fortune by a wealthy marriage with a lady whom he dearly loved, whose father, that was lately dead, had left her sole heiress to a large estate; and that in her father's lifetime he used to visit at her house, when he thought he had observed this lady had sometimes from her eyes sent speechless messages, that seemed to say he would be no unwelcome suitor; but not having money to furnish himself with an appearance befitting the lover of so rich an heiress, he besought Antonio to add to the many favors he had shown him, by lending him three thousand ducats[9].

Bassanio

8 patrimony [ˈpætrɪmoʊni] (n.) 祖產
9 ducat [ˈdʌkət] (n.) 舊時流通於歐洲、價值不一的金銀幣

Antonio had no money by him at that time to lend his friend; but expecting soon to have some ships come home laden with merchandise, he said he would go to Shylock, the rich moneylender, and borrow the money upon the credit of those ships.

Antonio and Bassanio went together to Shylock, and Antonio asked the Jew to lend him three thousand ducats upon any interest he should require, to be paid out of the merchandise contained in his ships at sea.

On this, Shylock thought within himself: "If I can once catch him on the hip, I will feed fat the ancient grudge[10] I bear him, he hates our Jewish nation; he lends out money gratis[11]; and among the merchants he rails[12] at me and my well-earned bargains, which he calls interest. Cursed be my tribe if I forgive him!"

Antonio finding he was musing[13] within himself and did not answer, and being impatient for the money, said: "Shylock, do you hear? Will you lend the money?"

10 grudge [grʌdʒ] (n.) 怨恨
11 gratis ['ɡretɪs] (adv.) 免費地
12 rail [reɪl] (v.) 抱怨；責罵
13 muse ['mjuːz] (v.) 沈思

🎧 24 To this question the Jew replied: "Signior Antonio, on the Rialto many a time and often you have railed at me about my moneys and my usuries, and I have borne it with a patient shrug, for sufferance is the badge[14] of all our tribe; and then you have called me unbeliever, cut-throat dog, and spit upon my Jewish garments, and spurned[15] at me with your foot, as if I was a cur[16]. Well, then, it now appears you need my help, and you come to me, and say, 'Shylock, lend me moneys.' Has a dog money? Is it possible a cur should lend three thousand ducats? Shall I bend low and say, 'Fair sir, you spit upon me on Wednesday last, another time you called me dog, and for these courtesies I am to lend you moneys.'"

Antonio replied: "I am as like to call you so again, to spit on you again, and spurn you, too. If you will lend me this money, lend it not to me as to a friend, but rather lend it to me as to an enemy, that, if I break, you may with better face exact the penalty."

"Why, look you," said Shylock, "how you storm! I would be friends with you and have your love. I will forget the shames you have put upon me. I will supply your wants and take no interest for my money."

14 badge [bædʒ] (n.) 象徵；代表

15 spurn [spɜːrn] (v.) 一腳踢開；輕蔑地拒絕

16 cur [kɜːr] (n.) 行為卑劣者；野狗

This seemingly kind offer greatly surprised Antonio; and then Shylock, still pretending kindness and that all he did was to gain Antonio's love, again said he would lend him the three thousand ducats, and take no interest for his money; only Antonio should go with him to a lawyer and there sign in merry sport a bond[17], that if he did not repay the money by a certain day, he would forfeit[18] a pound of flesh, to be cut off from any part of his body that Shylock pleased.

"Content," said Antonio, "I will sign to this bond, and say there is much kindness in the Jew."

Bassanio said Antonio should not sign to such a bond for him; but still Antonio insisted that he would sign it, for that before the day of payment came, his ships would return laden with many times the value of the money.

Shylock, hearing this debate, exclaimed: "O, father Abraham, what suspicious people these Christians are! Their own hard dealings teach them to suspect the thoughts of others. I pray you tell me this, Bassanio: if he should break his day, what should I gain by the exaction of the forfeiture? A pound of man's flesh, taken from a man, is not so estimable[19], nor profitable, neither, as the flesh of mutton or beef. I say, to buy his favor I offer this friendship: if he will take it, so; if not, adieu."

At last, against the advice of Bassanio, who, notwithstanding all the Jew had said of his kind intentions, did not like his friend should run the hazard[20] of this shocking penalty for his sake, Antonio signed the bond, thinking it really was (as the Jew said) merely in sport.

17 bond [bɑːnd] (n.) 字據
18 forfeit [ˈfɔːrfit] (v.) 喪失
19 estimable [ˈestɪməbəl] (a.) 有價值的
20 hazard [ˈhæzərd] (n.) 危險

Portia

The rich heiress that Bassanio wished to marry lived near Venice, at a place called Belmont. Her name was Portia, and in the graces of her person and her mind she was nothing inferior to that Portia, of whom we read, who was Cato's daughter and the wife of Brutus.

Bassanio being so kindly supplied with money by his friend Antonio, at the hazard of his life, set out for Belmont with a splendid train and attended by a gentleman of the name of Gratiano.

Bassanio proving successful in his suit, Portia in a short time consented to accept of him for a husband.

Bassanio confessed to Portia that he had no fortune and that his high birth and noble ancestry was all that he could boast of; she, who loved him for his worthy qualities and had riches enough not to regard wealth in a husband, answered, with a graceful modesty, that she would wish herself a thousand times more fair, and ten thousand times more rich, to be more worthy of him; and then the accomplished Portia prettily dispraised herself, and said she was an unlessoned girl, unschooled, unpracticed, yet not so old but that she could learn, and that she would commit her gentle spirit to be directed and governed by him in all things; and she said:

27

"Myself and what is mine to you and yours is now converted [21]. But yesterday, Bassanio, I was the lady of this fair mansion, queen of myself, and mistress over these servants; and now this house, these servants, and myself, are yours, my lord; I give them with this ring," presenting a ring to Bassanio.

Bassanio was so overpowered with gratitude and wonder at the gracious manner in which the rich and noble Portia accepted of a man of his humble fortunes that he could not express his joy and reverence [22] to the dear lady who so honored him, by anything but broken words of love and thankfulness; and, taking the ring, he vowed never to part with it.

Gratiano and Nerissa, Portia's waiting-maid, were in attendance upon their lord and lady, when Portia so gracefully promised to become the obedient wife of Bassanio; and Gratiano, wishing Bassanio and the generous lady joy, desired permission to be married at the same time.

"With all my heart, Gratiano," said Bassanio, "if you can get a wife."

Portia, Bassanio, Gratiano and Nerissa

21 convert [kənˈvɜːrt] (v.) 使轉變
22 reverence [ˈrevərəns] (n.) 尊敬；敬畏之情

28

Gratiano then said that he loved the Lady Portia's fair waiting-gentlewoman, Nerissa, and that she had promised to be his wife if her lady married Bassanio. Portia asked Nerissa if this was true.

Nerissa replied: "Madam, it is so, if you approve of it."

Portia willingly consenting[23], Bassanio pleasantly said: "Then our wedding-feast shall be much honored by your marriage, Gratiano."

The happiness of these lovers was sadly crossed[24] at this moment by the entrance of a messenger, who brought a letter from Antonio containing fearful tidings[25].

When Bassanio read Antonio's letter, Portia feared it was to tell him of the death of some dear friend, he looked so pale; and, enquiring what was the news which had so distressed him, he said: "Oh, sweet Portia, here are a few of the unpleasantest words that ever blotted[26] paper! Gentle lady, when I first imparted[27] my love to you, I freely told you all the wealth I had ran in my veins; but I should have told you that I had less than nothing, being in debt."

Bassanio then told Portia what has been here related[28], of his borrowing the money of Antonio, and of Antonio's procuring[29] it of Shylock the Jew, and of the bond by which Antonio had engaged to forfeit a pound of flesh, if it was not repaid by a certain day: and then Bassanio read Antonio's letter, the words of which were:

'Sweet Bassanio, my ships are all lost, my bond to the Jew is forfeited, and since in paying it is impossible I should live, I could wish to see you at my death; notwithstanding, use your pleasure. If your love for me do not persuade you to come, let not my letter.'

23 consent [kən'sent] (v.) 同意
24 cross [krɔːs] (v.) 反對；阻礙；越過
25 tidings ['taɪdɪŋz] (n.) 消息；音信
26 blot [blɑːt] (v.) 在（紙上）弄點墨水
27 impart [ɪm'pɑːrt] (v.) 通知；告知
28 relate [rɪ'leɪt] (v.) 講述
29 procure [pro'kjʊr] (v.) 獲得；取得

"Oh, my dear love," said Portia, "despatch[30] all business and begone; you shall have gold to pay the money twenty times over, before this kind friend shall lose a hair by my Bassanio's fault; and as you are so dearly bought, I will dearly love you."

Portia then said she would be married to Bassanio before he set out, to give him a legal right to her money; and that same day they were married, and Gratiano was also married to Nerissa; and Bassanio and Gratiano, the instant they were married, set out in great haste for Venice, where Bassanio found Antonio in prison.

The day of payment being past, the cruel Jew would not accept of the money which Bassanio offered him, but insisted upon having a pound of Antonio's flesh. A day was appointed to try this shocking cause before the Duke of Venice, and Bassanio awaited in dreadful suspense the event of the trial.

---

30 despatch [dɪˈspætʃ] (v.) 迅速結束；打發；調遣

When Portia parted with her husband, she spoke cheeringly to him and bade him bring his dear friend along with him when he returned; yet she feared it would go hard with Antonio, and when she was left alone, she began to think and consider within herself if she could by any means be instrumental[31] in saving the life of her dear Bassanio's friend. And notwithstanding when she wished to honor her Bassanio, she had said to him, with such a meek[32] and wifelike grace, that she would submit in all things to be governed by his superior wisdom, yet being now called forth into action by the peril[33] of her honored husband's friend, she did nothing doubt her own powers, and by the sole guidance of her own true and perfect judgement at once resolved to go herself to Venice and speak in Antonio's defence.

Portia had a relation who was a counselor in the law; to this gentleman, whose name was Bellario, she wrote, and, stating the case to him, desired his opinion, and that with his advice he would also send her the dress worn by a counselor.

---

31 instrumental [ˌɪnstrəˈmentəl] (a.) 有幫助的
32 meek [miːk] (a.) 溫順的
33 peril [ˈperəl] (n.) 危險

When the messenger returned, he brought letters from Bellario of advice how to proceed, and also everything necessary for her equipment.

Portia dressed herself and her maid Nerissa in men's apparel[34], and putting on the robes of a counselor, she took Nerissa along with her as her clerk; and setting out immediately, they arrived at Venice on the very day of the trial.

The cause was just going to be heard before the Duke and senators of Venice in the senate-house, when Portia entered this high court of justice and presented a letter from Bellario, in which that learned counselor wrote to the duke, saying he would have come himself to plead[35] for Antonio but that he was prevented by sickness, and he requested that the learned young doctor Balthasar (so he called Portia) might be permitted to plead in his stead[36].

This the Duke granted, much wondering at the youthful appearance of the stranger, who was prettily disguised by her counselor's robes and her large wig.

34 apparel [əˈpærəl] (n.) 服裝
35 plead [pliːd] (v.) 為某人辯護
36 stead [sted] (n.) 代替

And now began this important trial. Portia looked around her and she saw the merciless Jew; and she saw Bassanio, but he knew her not in her disguise. He was standing beside Antonio, in an agony[37] of distress and fear for his friend.

The importance of the arduous[38] task Portia had engaged in gave this tender lady courage, and she boldly proceeded in the duty she had undertaken to perform. And first of all she addressed herself to Shylock; and allowing that he had a right by the Venetian law to have the forfeit expressed in the bond, she spoke so sweetly of the noble quality of MERCY as would have softened any heart but the unfeeling Shylock's, saying that it dropped as the gentle rain from heaven upon the place beneath; and how mercy was a double blessing, it blessed him that gave and him that received it; and how it became monarchs[39] better than their crowns, being an attribute[40] of God himself; and that earthly power came nearest to God's in proportion as mercy tempered[41] justice; and she bade Shylock remember that as we all pray for mercy, that same prayer should teach us to show mercy.

37 agony ['ægəni] (n.) 極大的痛苦

38 arduous ['ɑːrdʒuəs] (a.) 艱鉅的；困難的

39 monarch ['mɑːnərk] (n.) 君主

40 attribute [ə'trɪbjuːt] (n.) 性質；屬性

41 temper ['tempər] (v.) 調和；使緩和；使軟化

Shylock only answered her by desiring to have the penalty forfeited in the bond.

"Is he not able to pay the money?" asked Portia.

Bassanio then offered the Jew the payment of the three thousand ducats as many times over as he should desire; which Shylock refusing, and still insisting upon having a pound of Antonio's flesh, Bassanio begged the learned young counselor would endeavor to wrest [42] the law a little, to save Antonio's life. But Portia gravely answered that laws once established must never be altered.

Shylock, hearing Portia say that the law might not be altered, it seemed to him that she was pleading in his favor, and he said: "A Daniel is come to judgment! O wise young judge, how I do honor you! How much elder are you than your looks!"

Portia now desired Shylock to let her look at the bond; and when she had read it she said: "This bond is forfeited, and by this the Jew may lawfully claim a pound of flesh, to be by him cut off nearest Antonio's heart." Then she said to Shylock, "Be merciful; take the money and bid me tear the bond."

42 wrest [rest] (v.) 歪曲；曲解

But no mercy would the cruel Shylock show; and he said, "By my soul, I swear there is no power in the tongue of man to alter me."

"Why, then, Antonio," said Portia, "you must prepare your bosom for the knife." And while Shylock was sharpening a long knife with great eagerness to cut off the pound of flesh, Portia said to Antonio, "Have you anything to say?"

Antonio with a calm resignation[43] replied that he had but little to say, for that he had prepared his mind for death. Then he said to Bassanio: "Give me your hand, Bassanio! Fare you well! Grieve not that I am fallen into this misfortune for you. Commend me to your honorable wife and tell her how I have loved you!"

Bassanio in the deepest affliction[44] replied: "Antonio, I am married to a wife who is as dear to me as life itself; but life itself, my wife, and all the world are not esteemed with me above your life. I would lose all, I would sacrifice all to this devil here, to deliver[45] you."

Portia hearing this, though the kind-hearted lady was not at all offended with her husband for expressing the love he owed to so true a friend as Antonio in these strong terms, yet could not help answering: "Your wife would give you little thanks, if she were present, to hear you make this offer."

And then Gratiano, who loved to copy what his lord did, thought he must make a speech like Bassanio's, and he said, in Nerissa's hearing, who was writing in her clerk's dress by the side of Portia: "I have a wife whom I protest I love. I wish she were in heaven if she could but entreat[46] some power there to change the cruel temper of this currish Jew."

"It is well you wish this behind her back, else you would have but an unquiet house," said Nerissa.

Shylock now cried out impatiently: "We trifle time. I pray pronounce the sentence."

43 resignation [ˌrezɪgˈneɪʃən] (n.) 聽任；順從
44 affliction [əˈflɪkʃən] (n.) 痛苦
45 deliver [dɪˈlɪvər] (v.) 解救；釋放
46 entreat [ɪnˈtriːt] (v.) 懇求

And now all was awful expectation in the court, and every heart was full of grief for Antonio.

Portia asked if the scales were ready to weigh the flesh; and she said to the Jew, "Shylock, you must have some surgeon by, lest he bleed to death."

Shylock, whose whole intent was that Antonio should bleed to death, said, "It is not so named in the bond."

Portia replied: "It is not so named in the bond, but what of that? It were good you did so much for charity."

To this all the answer Shylock would make was, "I cannot find it; it is not in the bond."

"Then," said Portia, "a pound of Antonio's flesh is thine. The law allows it and the court awards it. And you may cut this flesh from off his breast. The law allows it and the court awards it."

Again Shylock exclaimed: "O wise and upright[47] judge! A Daniel is come to judgment!" And then he sharpened his long knife again, and looking eagerly on Antonio, he said, "Come, prepare!"

"Tarry[48] a little, Jew," said Portia. "There is something else. This bond here gives you no drop of blood; the words expressly are, 'a pound of flesh.' If in the cutting off the pound of flesh you shed one drop of Christian blood, your lands and goods are by the law to be confiscated[49] to the state of Venice."

---

47 upright ['ʌpraɪt] (a.) 正直的
48 tarry ['tæri] (v.) 停留；逗留
49 confiscate ['kɔ:nfɪskeɪt] (v.) 充公；沒收

Now as it was utterly impossible for Shylock to cut off the pound of flesh without shedding some of Antonio's blood, this wise discovery of Portia's, that it was flesh and not blood that was named in the bond, saved the life of Antonio; and all admiring the wonderful sagacity[50] of the young counselor who had so happily thought of this expedient[51], plaudits[52] resounded from every part of the senate-house; and Gratiano exclaimed, in the words which Shylock had used: "O wise and upright judge! Mark, Jew, a Daniel is come to judgment!"

Shylock, finding himself defeated in his cruel intent, said, with a disappointed look, that he would take the money. And Bassanio, rejoiced beyond measure at Antonio's unexpected deliverance, cried out: "Here is the money!"

But Portia stopped him, saying: "Softly; there is no haste. The Jew shall have nothing but the penalty. Therefore prepare, Shylock, to cut off the flesh; but mind you shed no blood; nor do not cut off more nor less than just a pound; be it more or less by one poor scruple[53], nay, if the scale turn but by the weight of a single hair, you are condemned[54] by the laws of Venice to die, and all your wealth is forfeited to the senate."

50 sagacity [sə'gæsɪti] (n.) 精明；睿智

51 expedient [ɪk'spiːdiənt] (n.) 權宜之計

52 plaudit ['plɔːdɪt] (n.) 喝采；鼓掌

53 scruple ['skruːpəl] (n.) 微量；重量單位（等於 1.3 克）

54 condemn [kən'dem] (v.) 判罪；處刑

"Give me my money and let me go," said Shylock.

"I have it ready," said Bassanio. "Here it is."

Shylock was going to take the money, when Portia again stopped him, saying: "Tarry, Jew. I have yet another hold upon you. By the laws of Venice, your wealth is forfeited to the state for having conspired[55] against the life of one of its citizens, and your life lies at the mercy of the duke; therefore, down on your knees and ask him to pardon you."

The duke then said to Shylock: "That you may see the difference of our Christian spirit, I pardon you your life before you ask it. Half your wealth belongs to Antonio, the other half comes to the state."

The generous Antonio then said that he would give up his share of Shylock's wealth, if Shylock would sign a deed to make it over at his death to his daughter and her husband; for Antonio knew that the Jew had an only daughter who had lately married against his consent to a young Christian named Lorenzo, a friend of Antonio's, which had so offended Shylock that he had disinherited her.

---

55 conspire [kən'spaɪr] (v.) 密謀；陰謀

Shylock's daughter

The Jew agreed to this; and being thus disappointed in his revenge and despoiled[56] of his riches, he said: "I am ill. Let me go home. Send the deed after me, and I will sign over half my riches to my daughter."

"Get thee gone, then," said the duke, "and sign it; and if you repent[57] your cruelty and turn Christian, the state will forgive you the fine of the other half of your riches."

The duke now released Antonio and dismissed the court. He then highly praised the wisdom and ingenuity[58] of the young counselor and invited him home to dinner.

Portia, who meant to return to Belmont before her husband, replied, "I humbly thank your grace, but I must away directly."

The duke said he was sorry he had not leisure to stay and dine with him, and, turning to Antonio, he added, "Reward this gentleman; for in my mind you are much indebted to him."

56 despoil [dɪ'spɔɪl] (v.) 奪取；掠奪
57 repent [rɪ'pent] (v.) 悔悟；痛悔
58 ingenuity [ˌɪndʒə'njuːəti] (n.) 靈巧；機靈

The duke and his senators left the court; and then Bassanio said to Portia: "Most worthy gentleman, I and my friend Antonio have by your wisdom been this day acquitted[59] of grievous penalties, and I beg you will accept of the three thousand ducats due unto the Jew."

"And we shall stand indebted to you over and above," said Antonio, "in love and service evermore."

Portia could not be prevailed[60] upon to accept the money. But upon Bassanio still pressing her to accept of some reward, she said: "Give me your gloves. I will wear them for your sake." And then Bassanio taking off his gloves, she espied[61] the ring which she had given him upon his finger. Now it was the ring the wily[62] lady wanted to get from him to make a merry jest when she saw her Bassanio again, that made her ask him for his gloves; and she said, when she saw the ring, "And for your love, I will take this ring from you."

Bassanio was sadly distressed that the counselor should ask him for the only thing he could not part with, and he replied, in great confusion, that he could not give him that ring, because it was his wife's gift and he had vowed never to part with it; but that he would give him the most valuable ring in Venice, and find it out by proclamation[63].

On this Portia affected to be affronted[64], and left the court, saying, "You teach me, sir, how a beggar should be answered."

"Dear Bassanio," said Antonio, "let him have the ring. Let My love and the great service he has done for me be valued against your wife's displeasure."

Bassanio, ashamed to appear so ungrateful, yielded, and sent Gratiano after Portia with the ring; and then the "clerk" Nerissa, who had also given Gratiano a ring, she begged his ring, and Gratiano (not choosing to be outdone in generosity by his lord) gave it to her.

---

59 acquit [ə'kwɪt] (v.) 宣告某人無罪
60 prevail [prɪ'veɪl] (v.) 勸導
61 espy [ɪs'paɪ] (v.) 看見；發現
62 wily ['waɪli] (a.) 多智謀的；狡詐的
63 proclamation [ˌprɔːklə'meɪʃən] (n.) 宣告；公布
64 affront [ə'frʌnt] (v.) 使當眾難堪

And there was laughing among these ladies to think, when they got home, how they would tax[65] their husbands with giving away their rings and swear that they had given them as a present to some woman.

Portia, when she returned, was in that happy temper of mind which never fails to attend the consciousness of having performed a good action. Her cheerful spirits enjoyed everything she saw: the moon never seemed to shine so bright before; and when that pleasant moon was hid behind a cloud, then a light which she saw from her house at Belmont as well pleased her charmed fancy, and she said to Nerissa: "That light we see is burning in my hall. How far that little candle throws its beams! So shines a good deed in a naughty world." And hearing the sound of music from her house, she said, "Methinks that music sounds much sweeter than by day."

And now Portia and Nerissa entered the house, and, dressing themselves in their own apparel, they awaited the arrival of their husbands, who soon followed them with Antonio; and Bassanio presenting his dear friend to the Lady Portia, the congratulations and welcomings of that lady were hardly over when they perceived Nerissa and her husband quarreling in a corner of the room.

65 tax [tæks] (v.) 指控;責備

"A quarrel already?" said Portia. "What is the matter?"

Gratiano replied, "Lady, it is about a paltry[66] gilt[67] ring that Nerissa gave me, with words upon it like the poetry on a cutler's[68] knife: 'Love me, and leave me not.'"

"What does the poetry or the value of the ring signify?" said Nerissa. "You swore to me when I gave it to you, that you would keep it till the hour of death; and now you say you gave it to the lawyer's clerk. I know you gave it to a woman."

"By this hand," replied Gratiano, "I gave it to a youth, a kind of boy, a little scrubbed[69] boy, no higher than yourself; he was clerk to the young counselor that by his wise pleading saved Antonio's life. This prating[70] boy begged it for a fee, and I could not for my life deny him."

---

66 paltry ['pɔːltri] (a.) 無價值的；微不足道的
67 gilt [gɪlt] (n.) 鍍金材料
68 cutler ['kʌtlər] (n.) 刀匠
69 scrubbed [skrʌbd] (a.) 矮小的
70 prating ['prætɪŋ] (a.) 喋喋不休的

42

Portia said: "You were to blame, Gratiano, to part with your wife's first gift. I gave my Lord Bassanio a ring, and I am sure he would not part with it for all the world."

Gratiano, in excuse for his fault, now said, "My Lord Bassanio gave his ring away to the counselor, and then the boy, his clerk, that took some pains in writing, he begged my ring."

Portia, hearing this, seemed very angry and reproached Bassanio for giving away her ring; and she said Nerissa had taught her what to believe, and that she knew some woman had the ring. Bassanio was very unhappy to have so offended his dear lady, and he said with great earnestness:

"No, by my honor, no woman had it, but a civil doctor who refused three thousand ducats of me and begged the ring, which when I denied him, he went displeased away. What could I do, sweet Portia? I was so beset[71] with shame for my seeming ingratitude that I was forced to send the ring after him. Pardon me, good lady. Had you been there, I think you would have begged the ring of me to give the worthy doctor."

"Ah!" said Antonio, "I am the unhappy cause of these quarrels."

Portia bid Antonio not to grieve at that, for that he was welcome notwithstanding; and then Antonio said: "I once did lend my body for Bassanio's sake; and but for him to whom your husband gave the ring, I should have now been dead. I dare be bound again, my soul upon the forfeit, your lord will never more break his faith with you."

"Then you shall be his surety[72]," said Portia. "Give him this ring and bid him keep it better than the other."

When Bassanio looked at this ring, he was strangely surprised to find it was the same he gave away; and then Portia told him how she was the young counselor, and Nerissa was her clerk; and Bassanio found, to his unspeakable wonder and delight, that it was by the noble courage and wisdom of his wife that Antonio's life was saved.

---

71 beset [bɪˈset] (v.) 包圍
72 surety [ˈsuəti] (n.) 保證人

43

And Portia again welcomed Antonio, and gave him letters which by some chance had fallen into her hands, which contained an account of Antonio's ships, that were supposed lost, being safely arrived in the harbor.

So these tragical beginnings of this rich merchant's story were all forgotten in the unexpected good fortune which ensued[73]; and there was leisure to laugh at the comical adventure of the rings, and the husbands that did not know their own wives, Gratiano merrily swearing, in a sort of rhyming speech, that—

While he lived, he'd fear no other thing
So sore, as keeping safe Nerissa's ring.

---

73 ensue [ɪnˈsuː] (v.) 隨之發生

《威尼斯商人》名句選

Shylock　　Go to then, you come to me, and you say,
　　　　　"Shylock, we would have moneys." You say so...
　　　　　Shall I bend low and in a bondman's key,
　　　　　With bated breath and whispering
　　　　　humbleness, Say this:
　　　　　"Fair sir, you spit on me Wednesday last,
　　　　　You spurn'd me such a day, another time
　　　　　You call'd me dog; and for these courtesies
　　　　　I'll lend you thus much moneys?"
　　　　　(I, iii, 115-16, 123-29)

賽拉客　　於是，您跑來找我，您說，
　　　　　「賽拉客，我們要幾個錢。」您說了……
　　　　　我該不該哈著腰，像個奴才，
　　　　　低聲下氣恭恭敬敬地，說道：
　　　　　「可愛的先生，您上星期三吐我口水，
　　　　　還有一天您用腳踢我，另外一次
　　　　　您喊我狗；為了報答這些厚愛，
　　　　　所以我應該借給您這麼多錢？」
　　　　　（第一幕，第三景，115-16 行，123-29 行）

Portia   The quality of mercy is not strain'd,
It droppeth as the gentle rain from heaven
Upon the place beneath. It is twice blest:
It blesseth him that gives and him that takes.
(IV, i, 184–87)

波兒榭   仁慈非出自於勉強，

它如甘霖從天而降；

仁慈是雙重的福份，

施主和受者都賜福。

（第四幕，第一景，184–87 行）

Shylock   Most learned judge, a sentence! Come prepare!
Portia   Tarry a little, there is something else.
This bond doth give thee here no jot of blood;
The words expressly are "a pound of flesh."
(IV, i, 304–7)

賽拉客   博學多識的法官，判得好！來，準備了！
波兒榭   且慢，尚有一事。

約上未允諾給你血，

僅寫明「一磅肉」。

（第四幕，第一景，304–7 行）

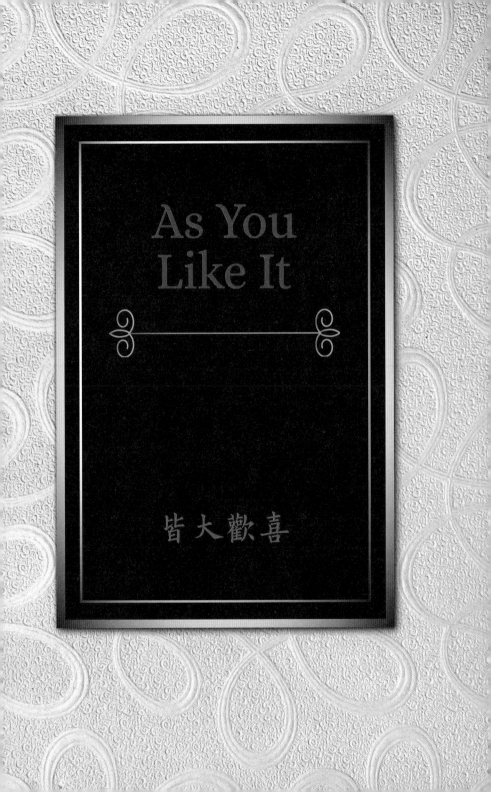

As You Like It

皆大歡喜

《皆大歡喜》導讀

歡慶喜劇

《皆大歡喜》一般推測的寫作年代為 1599–1600 年，此劇通常與《無事生非》及《第十二夜》並列為莎士比亞的三大歡慶喜劇（festive comedy）。

本劇有若干常見的莎劇主題，例如：由宮廷城市進入原始森林（如《仲夏夜之夢》）、善惡對比的兩兄弟（如《暴風雨》）、女扮男裝（如《威尼斯商人》、《第十二夜》）等。

本故事的來源有二：勞巨（Thomas Lodge）在 1590 年出版的《羅瑟琳》（*Rosalynde*），以及中古時期著名的暴力劇《嘉米林的故事》（*The Tale of Gamelyn*）。前者描寫田園生活中的浪漫愛情故事，後者描述弟弟如何向苛刻的兄長復仇。

《皆大歡喜》改寫當中的諸多情節，焦點放在羅莎琳與歐藍多的戀情，結局溫和。本劇劇情進展迅速，對白和情境環繞在田園生活和愛情故事。全劇的手法強調「內容重於語言，語言重於情節」，所以劇中沒有懸疑或明顯的衝突。劇末，所有的恩怨情仇都奇蹟似的被化解掉，最後結束流亡生涯，重返宮廷。

「命」與「運」

文藝復興時期的英國偏向從「命」（nature）和「運」（fortune）的互動來詮釋生命。《皆》劇中唯一令人感到緊張不安的，是惡劣運勢使得正義難以伸張，好人受苦，壞人享樂。

莎翁的戲劇通常呈現多元的主題和複雜的心理層面，人物性格通常好壞善惡兼雜，其所表現的戲劇張力，也有許多是源於內心欲望與外在命運的相互衝突。但本劇解決「命」與「運」之間衝突的方法卻教人啞然失笑：兩個反派角色最後痛改前非，搖身一變成為好人。天性邪惡的人只因「運」巧逢善人指導，從此悔過向善，因此沒有受到懲罰。

田園文學

本劇的特點之一是椏藤森林，使得全劇充滿濃厚的田園文學氣息。椏藤森林的名稱可能源於莎翁故鄉瓦維克（Warwick）附近的一個城鎮，這也是他母親椏藤（Mary Arden）的姓氏，也有可能是直接取用《羅瑟琳》中的地名阿登（Ardenne，這個法文就是英文的 Arden）。

在概念上，椏藤森林可能類似俠盜羅賓漢的「雪梧森林」（Sherwood Forest），也可能是《聖經》裡的「伊甸園」，或是文學傳統裡的田野「雅卡迪」（Arcadia）。這些地點象徵對理想世界的憧憬及嚮往。傳統的田園文學作品都將原野描寫為靜謐祥和之地，是遠離城鎮宮廷的庇護所。

DID HE NOT MORALISE THIS SPECTACLE?

這種文學傳統始於古希臘詩人希奧奎底斯（Theocritus）對鄉野的謳歌，古羅馬詩人維吉爾（Virgil）延續此風格，強調田園生活與都市生活的對比。

到了文藝復興時期，就演變為鄉村與都市互相敵對的狀態。不少與莎翁同期的作家也曾依循這項傳統，其中較為著名的就是史賓塞（Edmund Spenser）和席德尼爵士（Sir Philip Sidney）。

田園與城市的相對性

在典型的田園文學作品中，常可見到主人翁從城都或宮廷中遭放逐的情節。這些被放逐的人在重返故城之前，都會經歷一番閒適無爭的田園生活，並喜歡上此一生活方式，而自視為牧羊人。作品中常出現歌唱和討論，其中常見的討論內容如：鄉村與都市生活的優缺點；人類的藝術，究竟是美化還是破壞了自然？高貴的天性，是與生俱來還是後天培養而成？這些辯論的核心在於自然與人為的關係，亦即城市、制度、社會階級等，是否優於簡單純樸的自然景致。

也因為盛行這種討論，使得田園文學漸漸轉向社會批評。莎翁在《皆》劇中則同時表現了對田園文學的認同與批評。雖然劇中人物最後在椏藤森林得到重生，但其原因並不只是靠大自然治癒心靈的力量，人類的善良和慷慨也占有很大的成分。因此，除了自然的陶冶，人類也需要文明的教化，愛情、寬容、幽默、智慧等須和大自然互相結合，才能臻於和諧。

成熟的女主角

歐藍多出場時，是個天性高貴的純樸青年，但因不諳世事而參加角力賽。另一個顯示他人生閱歷不足的地方，是他在樹上到處刻著書本上讀來的十四行詩，這表現了純情癡心，卻不代表他了解愛情。要等到羅莎琳出現，他才能邁向更成熟階段。

羅莎琳就像許多莎劇的女主角一樣（如茱麗葉、《威尼斯商人》的波兒樹、《終成眷屬》的海倫娜），在心智與感情上都比情人成熟。羅莎琳採取理智務實的態度，使歐藍多避免陷入佩脫拉克式戀情（Petrarchan love）的窠臼，其主要特徵是以誇大而不著邊際的方式，歌頌詩人心目中完美的理想情人，而事實上卻沒有真正獲得心上人的回應。

羅莎琳是莎劇中最生動迷人的女主角之一。她是本劇中的第一女主角，卻大都以男性裝扮出現，就像波兒樹與《第十二夜》的菲兒拉一樣。她們之所以女扮男裝，主要是藉以避免危險、自我保護、追求愛情，或是取得社會中具有權力的性別地位。（但我們也不要忘記當時的女性角色一律由少年扮演，因此莎士比亞創造這些劇情，可說是因應社會風俗及演員特質的特殊安排。）

在這幾個女扮男裝的例子中，羅莎琳是最為複雜的一個。文藝復興時期的女孩在家順從父母，嫁出去之後順從丈夫。但羅莎琳因父親被放逐，叔叔又把她趕出宮外，所以她沒有男性監護人，凡事必須自立。另外，她雖女扮男裝，卻仍擁有典型的女性特質，例如對瑟梨兒坦承她愛上歐藍多，或是聽到歐藍多受傷後就馬上昏厥等等。

雌雄莫辨的議題

文藝復興時期的劇場傳統，更讓這種雌雄莫辨呈現萬花筒式的鏡像關係。她原由少男所飾演，卻必須在劇中化身為名叫嘉尼米的男性，爾後再還原為女性羅莎琳，而觀眾還是不會忘記她原是由「他」所扮演。（文藝復興時期受到希臘醫學的影響，認為男女的性特徵並沒有很大的差異，因此主要是從服裝及舉止上來辨別男女。）

羅莎琳化身成男性嘉尼米，凸顯了性別轉換和同性戀的議題。嘉尼米是希臘神話中同性戀的代表人物，在文藝復興時期則象徵年長男子的少年情人。或許有人會將嘉尼米與歐藍多的感情詮釋為同性戀，而且田園文學中也早有歌頌同性戀的傳統。史賓塞在《牧羊年曆》（*The Shepheardes Calender*）中就有類似的情節，而在 1580 年代的《深情牧羊人》（*The Affectionate Shepherd*）中，男主人翁更是大方地表白自己對年輕男子嘉尼米的愛意。

嘉尼米和歐藍多之間的情誼是否為同性戀，見仁見智。有些批評家認為，嘉尼米其實是提供歐藍多認識羅莎琳的階梯，讓他先從嘉尼米身上獲得同性友誼，待建立彼此信任的關係後，再進一步從羅莎琳身上獲得異性的愛情。就劇本的角度來看，也的確如此，但若以當時角色扮演的性別限制，還有莎士比亞選擇了嘉尼米這個名字來看，恐怕就沒有那麼單純了。

一般的評價

自十八世紀起，評論家似乎都認為《皆大歡喜》的寫作技巧並不好。英國作家強生（Samuel Johnson）認為此劇的結局過於匆促，失去陳述道德教育的機會；愛爾蘭劇作家蕭伯納（George Bernard Shaw, 1856–1950）半開玩笑地表示，這個劇本不過是剽竊通俗故事裡的劇情，所謂的「皆大歡喜」（As You Like It）不過是「皆我（莎士比亞）喜歡」（as I like it）罷了；英國導演布魯克（Peter Brook）看完此劇文本後，也向莎士比亞說「我不喜歡」（as I don't like it）；也有人認為此劇前後矛盾，而且許多問題到劇終時仍然沒有獲得解決。

本劇在莎士比亞死後一直到 1740 年才開始有演出紀錄，之後逐漸成為莎劇的常備劇目。十九世紀末，此劇移至戶外公演後，更是經常呈現圖畫般的景象。到了二十世紀，本劇因為同時呈現純真與嘲諷、浪漫與寫實，而同時吸引了喜好知識與夢想的觀眾。

《皆大歡喜》人物表

the duck	流放公爵	一位因弟弟篡位而被流放到森林裡的公爵
Rosalind	羅莎琳	公爵的獨生女,後來男扮女裝,化名嘉尼米(Ganymede)
Celia	瑟梨兒	費得烈公爵的女兒,後來喬裝成村姑,化名雅菱娜(Aliena)
Orlando	歐藍多	貴族出身,和羅莎琳邂逅相戀
Duke Frederick	費得烈公爵	逐兄篡位,流放公爵的弟弟
Oliver	歐力維	歐藍多的兄長,待弟甚苛
Adam	亞當	歐藍多忠實的老僕人

As You Like It

44 During the time that France was divided into provinces (or dukedoms[1], as they were called) there reigned in one of these provinces a usurper[2] who had deposed[3] and banished his elder brother, the lawful duke.

The duke who was thus driven from his dominions retired with a few faithful followers to the forest of Arden; and here the good duke lived with his loving friends, who had put themselves into a voluntary exile for his sake, while their land and revenues enriched the false usurper; and custom soon made the life of careless ease they led here more sweet to them than the pomp and uneasy splendor of a courtier's life.

---

1 dukedom [ˈduːkdəm] (n.) 公國
2 usurper [juːˈzɜːrpər] (n.) 篡奪者；霸占者
3 depose [dɪˈpouz] (v.) 迫使下台

Here they lived like the old Robin Hood of England, and to this forest many noble youths daily resorted⁴ from the court, and did fleet the time carelessly, as they did who lived in the golden age. In the summer they lay along under the fine shade of the large forest trees, marking the playful sports of the wild deer; and so fond were they of these poor dappled⁵ fools, who seemed to be the native inhabitants of the forest, that it grieved them to be forced to kill them to supply themselves with venison⁶ for their food.

4 resort [rɪˈzɔːrt] (v.) 經常去
5 dappled [ˈdæpəld] (a.) 斑紋的
6 venison [ˈvenɪsən] (n.) 鹿肉

45 When the cold winds of winter made the duke feel the change of his adverse fortune, he would endure it patiently, and say: "These chilling winds which blow upon my body are true counselors; they do not flatter, but represent truly to me my condition; and though they bite sharply, their tooth is nothing like so keen as that of unkindness and ingratitude. I find that howsoever men speak against adversity[7], yet some sweet uses are to be extracted[8] from it; like the jewel, precious for medicine, which is taken from the head of the venomous[9] and despised toad."

In this manner did the patient duke draw a useful moral from everything that he saw; and by the help of this moralizing turn, in that life of his, remote from public haunts, he could find tongues in trees, books in the running brooks, sermons[10] in stones, and good in everything.

---

7 adversity [ədˈvɜːrsɪti] (n.) 厄運；災難
8 extract [ɪkˈstrækt] (v.) 拔出
9 venomous [ˈvenəməs] (a.) 有毒的
10 sermon [ˈsɜːrmən] (n.) 說教；啟示

🎧 **46** The banished duke had an only daughter, named Rosalind, whom the usurper, Duke Frederick, when he banished her father, still retained in his court as a companion for his own daughter, Celia. A strict friendship subsisted[11] between these ladies, which the disagreement between their fathers did not in the least interrupt, Celia striving by every kindness in her power to make amends to Rosalind for the injustice of her own father in deposing the father of Rosalind; and whenever the thoughts of her father's banishment, and her own dependence on the false usurper, made Rosalind melancholy, Celia's whole care was to comfort and console her.

One day, when Celia was talking in her usual kind manner to Rosalind, saying, "I pray you, Rosalind, my sweet cousin, be merry," a messenger entered from the duke, to tell them that if they wished to see a wrestling-match, which was just going to begin, they must come instantly to the court before the palace; and Celia, thinking it would amuse Rosalind, agreed to go and see it.

---

11 subsist [səb'sɪst] (v.) 存在

Rosalind and Celia

In those times wrestling, which is only practised now by country clowns, was a favorite sport even in the courts of princes, and before fair ladies and princesses. To this wrestling-match, therefore, Celia and Rosalind went.

They found that it was likely to prove a very tragical sight; for a large and powerful man, who had been long practised in the art of wrestling and had slain many men in contests of this kind, was just going to wrestle with a very young man, who, from his extreme youth and inexperience in the art, the beholders all thought would certainly be killed.

When the duke saw Celia and Rosalind he said: "How now, daughter and niece, are you crept hither to see the wrestling? You will take little delight in it, there is such odds in the men. In pity to this young man, I would wish to persuade him from wrestling. Speak to him, ladies, and see if you can move him."

The ladies were well pleased to perform this humane office, and first Celia entreated the young stranger that he would desist from the attempt; and then Rosalind spoke so kindly to him, and with such feeling

consideration for the danger he was about to undergo, that, instead of being persuaded by her gentle words to forego his purpose, all his thoughts were bent to distinguish himself by his courage in this lovely lady's eyes.

He refused the request of Celia and Rosalind in such graceful and modest words that they felt still more concern for him; he concluded his refusal with saying: "I am sorry to deny such fair and excellent ladies anything. But let your fair eyes and gentle wishes go with me to my trial, wherein if I be conquered there is one shamed that was never gracious; if I am killed, there is one dead that is willing to die. I shall do my friends no wrong, for I have none to lament me; the world no injury, for in it I have nothing; for I only fill up a place in the world which may be better supplied when I have made it empty."

And now the wrestling-match began. Celia wished the young stranger might not be hurt; but Rosalind felt most for him. The friendless state which he said he was in, and that he wished to die, made Rosalind think that he was, like herself, unfortunate; and she pitied him so much, and so deep an interest she took in his danger while he was wrestling, that she might almost be said at that moment to have fallen in love with him.

The kindness shown this unknown youth by these fair and noble ladies gave him courage and strength, so that he performed wonders; and in the end completely conquered his antagonist, who was so much hurt that for a while he was unable to speak or move.

The Duke Frederick was much pleased with the courage and skill shown by this young stranger; and desired to know his name and parentage, meaning to take him under his protection.

The stranger said his name was Orlando, and that he was the youngest son of Sir Rowland de Boys.

Sir Rowland de Boys, the father of Orlando, had been dead some years; but when he was living he had been a true subject and dear friend of the banished duke; therefore, when Frederick heard Orlando was the son of his banished brother's friend, all his liking for this brave young man was changed into displeasure and he left the place in very ill humor. Hating to bear the very name of any of his brother's friends, and yet still admiring the valor of the youth, he said, as he went out, that he wished Orlando had been the son of any other man.

Rosalind was delighted to hear that her new favorite was the son of her father's old friend; and she said to Celia, "My father loved Sir Rowland de Boys, and if I had known this young man was his son I would have added tears to my entreaties before he should have ventured."

The ladies then went up to him and, seeing him abashed[12] by the sudden displeasure shown by the duke, they spoke kind and encouraging words to him; and Rosalind, when they were going away, turned back to speak some more civil things to the brave young son of her father's old friend, and taking a chain from off her neck, she said: "Gentleman, wear this for me. I am out of suits with fortune, or I would give you a more valuable present."

When the ladies were alone, Rosalind's talk being still of Orlando, Celia began to perceive her cousin had fallen in love with the handsome young wrestler, and she said to Rosalind: "Is it possible you should fall in love so suddenly?"

Rosalind replied, "The duke, my father, loved his father dearly."

"But," said Celia, "does it therefore follow that you should love his son dearly? For then I ought to hate him, for my father hated his father; yet do not hate Orlando."

12 abash [ə'bæʃ] (v.) 使羞愧不安
13 malice ['mælɪs] (n.) 惡意
14 irrevocable [ɪ'revəkəbəl] (a.) 不可挽回的

Frederick, being enraged at the sight of Sir Rowland de Boys' son, which reminded him of the many friends the banished duke had among the nobility, and having been for some time displeased with his niece because the people praised her for her virtues and pitied her for her good father's sake, his malice[13] suddenly broke out against her; and while Celia and Rosalind were talking of Orlando, Frederick entered the room and with looks full of anger ordered Rosalind instantly to leave the palace and follow her father into banishment, telling Celia, who in vain pleaded for her, that he had only suffered Rosalind to stay upon her account.

"I did not then," said Celia, "entreat you to let her stay, for I was too young at that time to value her; but now that I know her worth, and that we so long have slept together, rose at the same instant, learned, played, and eat together, I cannot live out of her company."

Frederick replied, "She is too subtle for you; her smoothness, her very silence, and her patience speak to the people, and they pity her. You are a fool to plead for her, for you will seem more bright and virtuous when she is gone; therefore open not your lips in her favor, for the doom which I have passed upon her is irrevocable[14]."

15 defray [dɪ'freɪ] (v.) 支付

When Celia found she could not prevail upon her father to let Rosalind remain with her, she generously resolved to accompany her; and, leaving her father's palace that night, she went along with her friend to seek Rosalind's father, the banished duke, in the forest of Arden.

Before they set out Celia considered that it would be unsafe for two young ladies to travel in the rich clothes they then wore; she therefore proposed that they should disguise their rank by dressing themselves like country maids. Rosalind said it would be a still greater protection if one of them was to be dressed like a man. And so it was quickly agreed on between them that, as Rosalind was the tallest, she should wear the dress of a young countryman, and Celia should be habited like a country lass, and that they should say they were brother and sister; and Rosalind said she would be called Ganymede, and Celia chose the name of Aliena.

In this disguise, and taking their money and jewels to defray[15] their expenses, these fair princesses set out on their long travel; for the forest of Arden was a long way off, beyond the boundaries of the duke's dominions.

The lady Rosalind (or Ganymede, as she must now be called) with her manly garb seemed to have put on a manly courage. The faithful friendship Celia had shown in accompanying Rosalind so many weary miles made the new brother, in recompense[16] for this true love, exert a cheerful spirit, as if he were indeed Ganymede, the rustic and stout[17]-hearted brother of the gentle village maiden, Aliena.

When at last they came to the forest of Arden they no longer found the convenient inns and good accommodations they had met with on the road, and, being in want of food and rest, Ganymede, who had so merrily cheered his sister with pleasant speeches and happy remarks all the way, now owned to Aliena that he was so weary he could find in his heart to disgrace his man's apparel[18] and cry like a woman; and Aliena declared she could go no farther; and then again Ganymede tried to recollect that it was a man's duty to comfort and console a woman, as the weaker vessel[19], and to seem courageous to his new sister, he said: "Come, have a good heart, my sister Aliena. We are now at the end of our travel, in the forest of Arden."

---

16 recompense ['rekəmpens] (n.) 報償
17 stout [staut] (a.) 堅決的；剛毅的
18 apparel [ə'pærəl] (n.) 服裝
19 vessel ['vesəl] (n.) 血管

🎧 53 But feigned manliness and forced courage would no longer support them; for, though they were in the forest of Arden, they knew not where to find the duke. And here the travel of these weary ladies might have come to a sad conclusion, for they might have lost themselves and perished for want of food, but, providentially, as they were sitting on the grass, almost dying with fatigue and hopeless of any relief, a countryman chanced to pass that way, and Ganymede once more tried to speak with a manly boldness, saying: "Shepherd, if love or gold can in this desert place procure[20] us entertainment[21], I pray you bring us where we may rest ourselves; for this young maid, my sister, is much fatigued with traveling, and faints for want of food."

The man replied that he was only a servant to a shepherd, and that his master's house was just going to be sold, and therefore they would find but poor entertainment; but that if they would go with him they should be welcome to what there was.

---

20 procure [prə'kjʊr] (v.) 促成；招致
21 entertainment [ˌentər'teɪnmənt] (n.) 招待；款待；飲食

They followed the man, the near prospect of relief giving them fresh strength, and bought the house and sheep of the shepherd, and took the man who conducted them to the shepherd's house to wait on them; and being by this means so fortunately provided with a neat cottage, and well supplied with provisions[22], they agreed to stay here till they could learn in what part of the forest the duke dwelt.

When they were rested after the fatigue of their journey, they began to like their new way of life, and almost fancied themselves the shepherd and shepherdess they feigned to be. Yet sometimes Ganymede remembered he had once been the same Lady Rosalind who had so dearly loved the brave Orlando because he was the son of old Sir Rowland, her father's friend; and though Ganymede thought that Orlando was many miles distant, even so many weary miles as they had traveled, yet it soon appeared that Orlando was also in the forest of Arden. And in this manner this strange event came to pass.

Orlando was the youngest son of Sir Rowland de Boys, who, when he died, left him (Orlando being then very young) to the care of his eldest brother, Oliver,

charging Oliver on his blessing to give his brother a good education and provide for him as became the dignity of their ancient house. Oliver proved an unworthy brother, and, disregarding the commands of his dying father, he never put his brother to school, but kept him at home untaught and entirely neglected.

22 provisions [prə'vɪʒənz] (n.)〔作複數形〕食物供應

But in his nature and in the noble qualities of his mind Orlando so much resembled his excellent father that, without any advantages of education, he seemed like a youth who had been bred with the utmost care; and Oliver so envied the fine person and dignified manners of his untutored brother that at last he wished to destroy him, and to effect this be set on people to persuade him to wrestle with the famous wrestler who, as has been before related, had killed so many men. Now it was this cruel brother's neglect of him which made Orlando say he wished to die, being so friendless.

When, contrary to the wicked hopes he had formed, his brother proved victorious, his envy and malice knew no bounds, and he swore he would burn the chamber where Orlando slept. He was overheard making his vow by one that had been an old and faithful servant to their father, and that loved Orlando because he resembled Sir Rowland. This old man went out to meet him when he returned from the duke's palace, and when he saw Orlando the peril his dear young master was in made him break out into these passionate exclamations:

"O my gentle master, my sweet master! O you memory of Old Sir Rowland! Why are you virtuous? Why are you gentle, strong, and valiant[23]? And why would you be so fond to overcome the famous wrestler? Your praise is come too swiftly home before you."

Orlando, wondering what all this meant, asked him what was the matter. And then the old man told him how his wicked brother, envying the love all people bore him, and now hearing the fame he had gained by his victory in the duke's palace, intended to destroy him by setting fire to his chamber that night, and in conclusion advised him to escape the danger he was in by instant flight; and knowing Orlando had no money, Adam (for that was the good old man's name) had brought out with him his own little hoard[24], and he said: "I have five hundred crowns, the thrifty[25] hire I saved under your father and laid by to be provision for me when my old limbs should become unfit for service. Take that, and He that doth the ravens feed be comfort to my age! Here is the gold. All this I give to you. Let me be your servant; though I look old I will do the service of a younger man in all your business and necessities."

23 valiant ['væliənt] (a.) 勇敢的
24 hoard [hɔːrd] (n.) 貯藏的錢財
25 thrifty ['θrɪfti] (a.) 節儉的

"O good old man!" said Orlando, "how well appears in you the constant service of the old world! You are not for the fashion of these times. We will go along together, and before your youthful wages are spent I shall light upon some means for both our maintenance."

Together, then, this faithful servant and his loved master set out; and Orlando and Adam traveled on, uncertain what course to pursue, till they came to the forest of Arden, and there they found themselves in the same distress for want of food that Ganymede and Aliena had been. They wandered on, seeking some human habitation, till they were almost spent with hunger and fatigue.

Adam at last said: "O my dear master, I die for want of food. I can go no farther!" He then laid himself down, thinking to make that place his grave, and bade his dear master farewell.

Orlando, seeing him in this weak state, took his old servant up in his arms and carried him under the shelter of some pleasant trees; and he said to him: "Cheerly, old Adam. Rest your weary limbs here awhile, and do not talk of dying!"

Orlando and Adam.

🎧 57 Orlando then searched about to find some food, and he happened to arrive at that part of the forest where the duke was; and he and his friends were just going to eat their dinner, this royal duke being seated on the grass, under no other canopy[26] than the shady covert[27] of some large trees.

Orlando, whom hunger had made desperate, drew his sword, intending to take their meat by force, and said: "Forbear[28] and eat no more. I must have your food!"

The duke asked him if distress had made him so bold or if he were a rude despiser of good manners.

On this Orlando said he was dying with hunger; and then the duke told him he was welcome to sit down and eat with them.

Orlando, hearing him speak so gently, put up his sword and blushed with shame at the rude manner in which he had demanded their food.

---

26 canopy [ˈkænəpi] (n.) 頂篷
27 covert [ˈkouvərt] (n.) 動物藏身的樹叢
28 forbear [ˈfɔːrber] (v.) 抑制；忍耐

"Pardon me, I pray you," said he. "I thought that all things had been savage here, and therefore I put on the countenance of stern command; but whatever men you are that in this desert, under the shade of melancholy boughs, lose and neglect the creeping hours of time, if ever you have looked on better days, if ever you have been where bells have knolled to church, if you have ever sat at any good man's feast, if ever from your eyelids you have wiped a tear and know what it is to pity or be pitied, may gentle speeches now move you to do me human courtesy!"

🎧 58 The duke replied: "True it is that we are men (as you say) who have seen better days, and though we have now our habitation in this wild forest, we have lived in towns and cities and have with holy bell been knolled to church, have sat at good men's feasts, and from our eyes have wiped the drops which sacred pity has engendered[29], therefore sit you down and take of our refreshment[30] as much as will minister to your wants."

"There is an old poor man," answered Orlando, "who has limped after me many a weary step in pure love, oppressed at once with two sad infirmities[31], age and hunger; till he be satisfied I must not touch a bit."

"Go, find him out and bring him hither," said the duke. "We will forbear to eat till you return."

Then Orlando went like a doe[32] to find its fawn[33] and give it food; and presently returned, bringing Adam in his arms.

And the duke said, "Set down your venerable[34] burthen[35], you are both welcome."

And they fed the old man and cheered his heart, and he revived and recovered his health and strength again.

The duke inquired who Orlando was; and when he found that he was the son of his old friend, Sir Rowland de Boys, he took him under his protection, and Orlando and his old servant lived with the duke in the forest.

Orlando arrived in the forest not many days after Ganymede and Aliena came there and (as has been before related) bought the shepherd's cottage.

Ganymede and Aliena were strangely surprised to find the name of Rosalind carved on the trees, and love-sonnets fastened to them, all addressed to Rosalind; and while they were wondering how this could be they met Orlando and they perceived the chain which Rosalind had given him about his neck.

29 engender [ɪn'dʒendər] (v.) 使產生；引起
30 refreshment [rɪ'freʃmənt] (n.) 提神的東西（尤指食物和飲料）
31 infirmity [ɪn'fɜːrmɪti] (n.) 疾病；弱點
32 doe [doʊ] (n.) 母鹿；雌兔
33 fawn [fɑːn] (n.) 麑；幼小梅花鹿
34 venerable ['venərəbəl] (a.) 可敬的
35 burthen ['bɜːrðən] (n.)〔文學用法〕負擔

🎧59 Orlando little thought that Ganymede was the fair Princess Rosalind who, by her noble condescension[36] and favor, had so won his heart that he passed his whole time in carving her name upon the trees and writing sonnets in praise of her beauty; but being much pleased with the graceful air of this pretty shepherd-youth, he entered into conversation with him, and he thought he saw a likeness in Ganymede to his beloved Rosalind, but that he had none of the dignified deportment[37] of that noble lady; for Ganymede assumed the forward[38] manners often seen in youths when they are between boys and men, and with much archness[39] and humor talked to Orlando of a certain lover, "who," said she, "haunts our forest, and spoils our young trees with carving Rosalind upon their barks; and he hangs odes upon hawthorns[40], and elegies[41] on brambles[42], all praising this same Rosalind. If I could find this lover, I would give him some good counsel that would soon cure him of his love."

36 condescension [ˌkɑːndɪˈsenʃən] (n.) 屈尊俯就
37 deportment [dɪˈpɔːrtmənt] (n.) 行為舉止
38 forward [ˈfɔːrwərd] (a.) 魯莽的；冒失的
39 archness [ˈɑːrtʃnəs] (n.) 淘氣
40 hawthorn [ˈhɑːθɔːrn] (n.) 山楂
41 elegy [ˈelɪdʒi] (n.) 哀歌
42 bramble [ˈbræmbəl] (n.) 荊棘

Orlando confessed that he was the fond lover of whom he spoke,, and asked Ganymede to give him the good counsel he talked Of. The remedy Ganymede proposed, and the counsel he gave him was that Orlando should come every day to the cottage where he and his sister Aliena dwelt. "And then," said Ganymede, "I will feign myself to be Rosalind, and you shall feign to court me in the same manner as you would do if I was Rosalind, and then I will imitate the fantastic ways of whimsical[43] ladies to their lovers, till I make you ashamed of your love; and this is the way I propose to cure you."

Orlando had no great faith in the remedy, yet he agreed to come every day to Ganymede's cottage and feign a playful courtship; and every day Orlando visited Ganymede and Aliena, and Orlando called the shepherd Ganymede his Rosalind, and every day talked over all the fine words and flattering compliments which young men delight to use when they court their mistresses. It does not appear, however, that Ganymede made any progress in curing Orlando of his love for Rosalind.

43 whimsical ['wɪmzɪkəl] (a.) 異想天開的

Though Orlando thought all this was but a sportive play (not dreaming that Ganymede was his very Rosalind), yet the opportunity it gave him of saying all the fond things he had in his heart pleased his fancy almost as well as it did Ganymede's, who enjoyed the secret jest in knowing these fine love-speeches were all addressed to the right person.

In this manner many days passed pleasantly on with these young people; and the good-natured Aliena, seeing it made Ganymede happy, let him have his own way and was diverted at the mock-courtship, and did not care to remind Ganymede that the Lady Rosalind had not yet made herself known to the duke her father, whose place of resort in the forest they had learned from Orlando.

Ganymede met the duke one day, and had some talk with him, and the duke asked of what parentage he came. Ganymede answered that he came of as good parentage as he did, which made the duke smile, for he did not suspect the pretty shepherd-boy came of royal lineage[44]. Then seeing the duke look well and happy, Ganymede was content to put off all further explanation for a few days longer.

44 lineage ['lɪnɪɪdʒ] (n.) 世系；血統

One morning, as Orlando was going to visit Ganymede, he saw a man lying asleep on the ground, and a large green snake had twisted itself about his neck. The snake, seeing Orlando approach, glided[45] away among the bushes. Orlando went nearer, and then he discovered a lioness lie crouching[46], with her head on the ground, with a catlike watch, waiting until the sleeping man awaked (for it is said that lions will prey on nothing that is dead or sleeping).

It seemed as if Orlando was sent by Providence[47] to free the man from the danger of the snake and lioness; but when Orlando looked in the man's face he perceived that the sleeper who was exposed to this double peril was his own brother Oliver, who had so cruelly used him and had threatened to destroy him by fire, and he was almost tempted to leave him a prey[48] to the hungry lioness; but brotherly affection and the gentleness of his nature soon overcame his first anger against his brother; and he drew his sword and attacked the lioness and slew her, and thus preserved his brother's life both from the venomous snake and from the furious lioness; but before Orlando could conquer the lioness she had torn one of his arms with her sharp claws.

While Orlando was engaged with the lioness, Oliver awaked, and, perceiving that his brother Orlando, whom he had so cruelly treated, was saving him from the fury of a wild beast at the risk of his own life, shame and remorse[49] at once seized him, and he repented[50] of his unworthy conduct and besought with many tears his brother's pardon for the injuries he had done him.

45 glide [glaɪd] (v.) 滑行
46 crouch [kraʊtʃ] (v.) 蹲伏
47 Providence [ˈprɑːvɪdəns] (n.)〔作大寫〕神；上帝
48 prey [preɪ] (n.) 被捕食的動物
49 remorse [rɪˈmɔːrs] (n.) 痛悔；自責
50 repent [rɪˈpent] (v.) 悔悟；悔改

Orlando rejoiced to see him so penitent[51], and readily forgave him. They embraced each other and from that hour Oliver loved Orlando with a true brotherly affection, though he had come to the forest bent on his destruction.

The wound in Orlando's arm having bled very much, he found himself too weak to go to visit Ganymede, and therefore he desired his brother to go and tell Ganymede, "whom," said Orlando, "I in sport do call my Rosalind," the accident which had befallen him.

Thither then Oliver went, and told to Ganymede and Aliena how Orlando had saved his life; and when he had finished the story of Orlando's bravery and his own providential[52] escape he owned to them that he was Orlando's brother who had so cruelly used him; and then he told them of their reconciliation[53].

The sincere sorrow that Oliver expressed for his offenses made such a lively impression on the kind heart of Aliena that she instantly fell in love with him; and Oliver observing how much she pitied the distress he told her he felt for his fault, he as suddenly fell in love with her.

But while love was thus stealing into the hearts of Aliena and Oliver, he was no less busy with Ganymede, who, hearing of the danger Orlando had been in, and that he was wounded by the lioness, fainted; and when he recovered he pretended that he had counterfeited[54] the swoon[55] in the imaginary character of Rosalind, and Ganymede said to Oliver: "Tell your brother Orlando how well I counterfeited a swoon."

But Oliver saw by the paleness of his complexion that he did really faint, and, much wondering at the weakness of the young man, he said, "Well, if you did counterfeit, take a good heart and counterfeit to be a man."

"So I do," replied Ganymede, truly, "but I should have been a woman by right."

---

51 penitent ['penɪtənt] (a.) 悔過的；懺悔的
52 providential [ˌprɑːvɪ'denʃəl] (a.) 天佑的
53 reconciliation [ˌrekənsɪli'eɪʃən] (n.) 和解
54 counterfeit ['kaʊntərfɪt] (v.) 偽造
55 swoon [swuːn] (n.) 昏厥

Oliver made this visit a very long one, and when at last he returned back to his brother he had much news to tell him; for, besides the account of Ganymede's fainting at the hearing that Orlando was wounded, Oliver told him how he had fallen in love with the fair shepherdess Aliena, and that she had lent a favorable ear to his suit, even in this their first interview; and he talked to his brother, as of a thing almost settled, that he should marry Aliena, saying that he so well loved her that he would live here as a shepherd and settle his estate[56] and house at home upon Orlando.

"You have my consent," said Orlando. "Let your wedding be tomorrow, and I will invite the duke and his friends. Go and persuade your shepherdess to agree to this. She is now alone, for, look, here comes her brother."

Oliver went to Aliena, and Ganymede, whom Orlando had perceived approaching, came to inquire after the health of his wounded friend.

56 estate [ɪ'steɪt] (n.) 財產

🎧 65 When Orlando and Ganymede began to talk over the sudden love which had taken place between Oliver and. Aliena, Orlando said he had advised his brother to persuade his fair shepherdess to be married on the morrow[57], and then he added how much he could wish to be married on the same day to his Rosalind.

Ganymede, who well approved of this arrangement, said that if Orlando really loved Rosalind as well as he professed to do, he should have his wish; for on the morrow he would engage to make Rosalind appear in her own person, and also that Rosalind should be willing to marry Orlando.

This seemingly wonderful event, which, as Ganymede was the Lady Rosalind, he could so easily perform, be pretended he would bring to pass by the aid of magic, which he said he had learned of an uncle who was a famous magician.

The fond lover Orlando, half believing and half doubting what he heard, asked Ganymede if he spoke in sober[58] meaning.

---

57 morrow ['mɔːrou] (n.) 翌日；次日
58 sober ['soubər] (a.) 認真的；嚴肅的

66

"By my life I do," said Ganymede; "therefore put on your best clothes, and bid the duke and your friends to your wedding, for if you desire to be married tomorrow to Rosalind, she shall be here."

The next morning, Oliver having obtained the consent of Aliena, they came into the presence of the duke, and with them also came Orlando.

They being all assembled to celebrate this double marriage, and as yet only one of the brides appearing, there was much of wondering and conjecture, but they mostly thought that Ganymede was making a jest of Orlando.

The duke, hearing that it was his own daughter that was to be brought in this strange way, asked Orlando if he believed the shepherd-boy could really do what he had promised; and while Orlando was answering that he knew not what to think, Ganymede entered and asked the duke, if he brought his daughter, whether he would consent to her marriage with Orlando.

"That I would," said the duke, "if I had kingdoms to give with her."

Ganymede then said to Orlando, "And you say you will marry her if I bring her here."

"That I would," said Orlando, "if I were king of many kingdoms."

Ganymede and Aliena then went out together, and, Ganymede throwing off his male attire[59], and being once more dressed in woman's apparel, quickly became Rosalind without the power of magic; and Aliena, changing her country garb[60] for her own rich clothes, was with as little trouble transformed into the lady Celia.

While they were gone, the duke said to Orlando that he thought the shepherd Ganymede very like his daughter Rosalind; and Orlando said he also had observed the resemblance.

---

59 attire [ə'taɪr] (n.) 服裝
60 garb [gɑːrb] (n.)（某種職業或民族特有的）服裝；裝束

67

They had no time to wonder how all this would end, for Rosalind and Celia, in their own clothes, entered, and, no longer pretending that it was by the power of magic that she came there, Rosalind threw herself on her knees before her father and begged his blessing.

It seemed so wonderful to all present that she should so suddenly appear, that it might well have passed for magic; but Rosalind would no longer trifle with her father, and told him the story of her banishment, and of her dwelling in the forest as a shepherd-boy, her cousin Celia passing as her sister.

The duke ratified[61] the consent he had already given to the marriage; and Orlando and Rosalind, Oliver and Celia, were married at the same time. And though their wedding could not be celebrated in this wild forest with any of the parade of splendor usual on such occasions, yet a happier wedding-day was never passed.

And while they were eating their venison under the cool shade of the pleasant trees, as if nothing should be wanting to complete the felicity[62] of this good duke and the true lovers, an unexpected messenger arrived to tell the duke the joyful news that his dukedom was restored to him.

61 ratify [ˈrætɪfaɪ] (v.) 批准
62 felicity [fɪˈlɪsɪti] (n.)〔文學用法〕幸福

The usurper, enraged at the flight of his daughter Celia, and hearing that every day men of great worth resorted to the forest of Arden to join the lawful duke in his exile, much envying that his brother should be so highly respected in his adversity, put himself at the head of a large force and advanced toward the forest, intending to seize his brother and put him with all his faithful followers to the sword; but by a wonderful interposition of Providence this bad brother was converted from his evil intention, for just as he entered the skirts of the wild forest he was met by an old religious man, a hermit, with whom he had much talk and who in the end completely turned his heart from his wicked design.

Thenceforward he became a true penitent, and resolved, relinquishing his unjust dominion, to spend the remainder of his days in a religious house. The first act of his newly conceived penitence was to send a messenger to his brother (as has been related) to offer to restore to him his dukedom, which he had usurped so long, and with it the lands and revenues of his friends, the faithful followers of his adversity.

This joyful news, as unexpected as it was welcome, came opportunely to heighten the festivity and rejoicings at the wedding of the princesses. Celia complimented her cousin on this good, fortune which had happened to the duke, Rosalind's father, and wished her joy very sincerely, though she herself was no longer heir to the dukedom, but by this restoration which her father had made, Rosalind was now the heir, so completely was the love of these two cousins unmixed with anything of jealousy or of envy.

The duke had now an opportunity of rewarding those true friends who had stayed with him in his banishment; and these worthy followers, though they had patiently shared his adverse fortune, were very well pleased to return in peace and prosperity, to the palace of their lawful duke.

《皆大歡喜》名句選

Duke Senior　Sweet are the uses of adversity,
　　　　　　Which, like the toad, ugly and venomous.
　　　　　　Wears yet a precious jewel in his head;
　　　　　　And this our life, exempt from public haunt,
　　　　　　Finds tongues in trees, books in the running
　　　　　　　　brooks,
　　　　　　Sermons in stones, and good in everything.
　　　　　　(II, i, 12–17)

公爵　　　　逆境有其甘美之效，
　　　　　　如蟾蜍雖醜陋有毒。
　　　　　　頭上卻頂珍貴寶石；
　　　　　　我們生活雖遠人煙，
　　　　　　卻可在林間聽話語，在溪流處尋得書本，
　　　　　　在石頭裡找到訓示，在事事之中都受益。

　　　　　　（第二幕，第一景，12-17 行）

Jaques   All the world's a stage,
And all the men and women merely players;
They have their exits and their entrances,
And one man in his time plays many parts,
His acts being seven ages.
(II, vii, 139–43)

杰奎思   整個世界即舞台，
一切男女皆演員；
都有退場有出場，
一生扮演多角色，
演出可分七階段。
(第二幕，第七景，139–43 行)

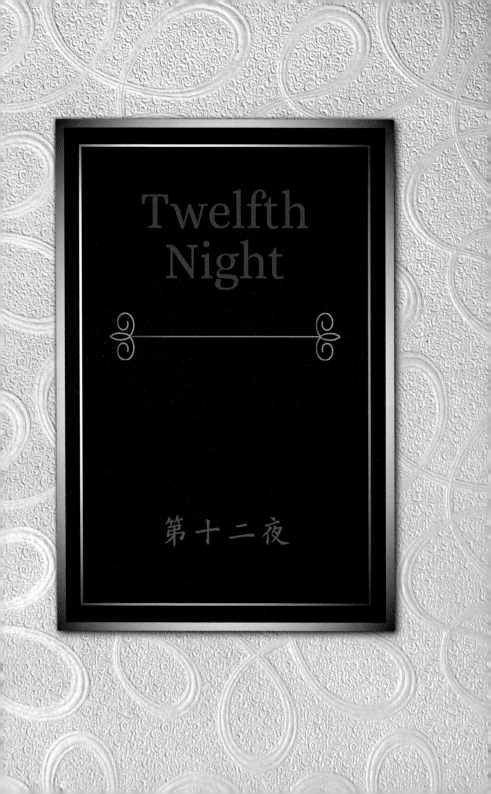

Twelfth Night

第十二夜

《第十二夜》導讀

第十二夜

莎翁的劇本中只有一部有兩個劇名，那就是《第十二夜》，又稱《隨心所欲》（*What You Will*）。「欲」（will）在伊麗莎白時期指的是「願望」，也指非理性的慾望或不受理智控制的激情。「第十二夜」指的則是基督教聖誕假期中的最後一夜，也就是一月六日的主顯節。耶穌誕生後，東方三博士（Magi）在這一天帶著禮物到伯利恆去參拜他。

到了伊麗莎白時期的英國，主顯節已經演變成狂歡作樂的日子，尤其主顯節晚上更是聖誕假期的高潮。當天，所有的規矩和秩序都會被暫時拋開，甚至反其道而行：年輕人可能會打扮成主教，在街上舉行荒謬可笑的宗教遊行；在嚴謹的道學家和信奉教條的法官常待的地方，到處可見各種諧擬的醜化行為；嚴肅的話題或事件會被拿來消遣取樂；在高等的學術校園裡，更是可見人們大肆作樂。

比起古羅馬異教徒每年十二月所舉行的農神節（Saturnalia），「第十二夜」的狂歡程度毫不遜色，連教會也難以制止。也因此，伊麗莎白時期的歡慶節日，以及散播異教徒、性解放等觀念的劇場，都遭到清教徒的反對。但在莎翁時代，因為伊麗莎白女王和詹姆士一世兩位君主都主張人們需要有適當的情緒發洩管道，因此都站在保護劇場的立場，加以贊助。

演出的歷史

《第十二夜》的紀錄最早出現在一位法學院學生莫寧翰（John Manningham）的日記裡。他在日記中提到：「筵席間，我們觀賞了一齣名為《第十二夜》的戲，內容就像《連環錯》、普勞特斯（Plautus）的《麥納克米》（Menaechmi），或是義大利的《騙局》（Inganni）。」這裡的筵席指的是 1602 年 2 月 2 日在中堂法學院（Middle Temple，為倫敦的一所法學院）舉辦的晚宴，但那一次的演出應該不是首演。

霍特森（Leslie Hotson）曾寫了一本書名叫《第十二夜的首夜》（First Night of "Twelfth Night"），內容就是描述該劇首演的狀況。霍特森相信，莎翁是奉皇室之命，因應義大利伯恰諾公爵歐析諾（Don Virginio Orsino）造訪英國，而寫下這個劇本，並在 1600 年的聖誕節後第十二夜（1 月 6 日）演出。但公爵來訪的消息在 12 月 26 日才傳至英國，若霍特森所言屬實，那就表示：在短短的十一、二天之內，莎翁就寫好劇本，所有演員就熟記台詞並完成排演。

霍特森還說，當時的觀眾都把《第十二夜》中的奧莉薇當成伊麗莎白女王，而歐析諾就是來訪的義大利公爵。這齣戲的目的就是要讚美遠道而來的貴賓，並奉承女王。但這種說法過於牽強，因為劇中的這兩個角色並不令人讚賞，而且伊麗莎白女王當時已經年過六旬，而公爵年僅二十八，且已成親。公爵還寫信給夫人，提到他在英國看了一齣載歌載舞的喜劇，至於那齣歌舞喜劇是否就是《第十二夜》，學者們仍未達成共識。

故事來源

莫寧翰所說無誤，義大利在 1537 年出版的喜劇《受騙者》（*Gl' Ingannati*），所描述的就是女扮男裝、錯認身分的故事，而且劇中還提到了主顯節。這個劇本在十六世紀出現了若干改編及譯本，其中一部英文版可能為莎翁所熟知，那就是瑞奇（Barnabe Rich）的小說《阿波羅紐與席拉》（*Apollonius and Silla*），收錄於 1581 年出版的《瑞奇揮別軍旅生涯》（*Rich's Farewell to His Military Profession*），而故事的來源就是普勞特斯的喜劇。

《阿波羅紐與席拉》是描述在一次船難後，席拉假扮成男僕進入阿波羅紐的宮殿，擔任他的傳情使者，向朱莉娜小姐求愛，不料朱莉娜卻愛上了席拉。待席拉的哥哥席歐出現後，在一夜之間讓朱莉娜懷了孕，但他之後卻離開，很久之後才回來，讓席拉陷入窘境。

這個故事雖然有許多情節都和《第十二夜》雷同，但是女扮男裝造成錯認的誤會，是一種常見的喜劇類型。這種傳統早在普勞特斯之前的米南德（Menander）時代（約西元前四世紀）就已經奠定，所以往往很難斷定某個故事的原作者，也因此無法確知莎翁到底是受了哪一部作品的影響。況且《阿波羅紐與席拉》或普勞特斯的喜劇都只注重情節變化，角色不帶感情，非常不同於《第十二夜》那種兼具歡樂及感傷的特質。

瘋癲的意味

本篇故事發生在伊利亞，讓故事不免帶有主顯節的癲狂意味，因為一般認為伊利亞人就有幾許瘋癲味。故事一開始就提到伊利亞的公爵歐析諾，因苦戀奧莉薇而變得消沈喪志，奧莉薇拒絕他，讓他終日沈溺在虛幻、浪漫、激情的夢想之中，失去了「男子氣概」。另一方面，奧莉薇誓言要為亡兄守喪七年，其間不取下面紗見任何人。這種不尋常的哀悼方式，彷彿是在與時間和記憶宣戰。但當她一見到菲兒拉假扮的男僕夏沙若，卻立刻違背了誓言，不可自拔地愛上夏沙若。

就喜劇而言，這種安排是很自然的，因為菲兒拉的攣生哥哥史裴俊最後一定會出現，繼而取代夏沙若。菲兒拉愛上歐析諾，卻不表明；奧莉薇愛上菲兒拉，菲兒拉也不急於澄清；安東尼誤認她為她哥哥，她也不加以解釋；她女扮男裝，也只是一種尋求方便的生存之道——一切靜待時間的安排。這種被動的態度為哥哥贏得了奧莉薇，拯救了安東尼，而且還使菲兒拉自己成為歐析諾夫人。在本劇中，「時間」具有了雙重意義：既帶來痛苦與悲傷，也帶來補償與幸福。

《第十二夜》的劇名，暗示著一個脫離現實的嘉年華世界，任何離奇的事件都不需要合理的解釋，所有不合常理的結局也都可以成立。譬如，這對長相酷似的攣生兄妹才分開三個月，重逢時卻得互相詢問，以確認身分；歐析諾在幾分鐘前還以為菲兒拉是個男僕，卻一下子就接受仍穿著男裝的她，並決定娶她為妻子；而奧莉薇嫁給完全陌生的史裴俊，竟一點也不以為忤。

歡慶喜劇

莎翁約在 1601 年完成《第十二夜》，當時已經寫過《仲夏夜之夢》、《無事生非》、《皆大歡喜》等喜劇，他透過趣味諷刺的手法，探討男女如何歷經同性或異性情誼而成為情侶。

在此階段，他也才剛完成《哈姆雷特》，心境上歷經了背叛、悲悼、癲狂、隔離，因此有許多評論家認為，《第十二夜》是莎翁最後一部、也是最好的一部歡慶喜劇（festive comedy），劇中捕捉到了文藝復興時期主顯節的精神。莎翁晚期雖將重心轉移至喜劇，但總是帶著痛苦悲傷或失落的味道。《第十二夜》雖然也有哀愁憂傷，但透過劇中的偽裝、愚行和幻想，降低了愁味。

因為悲喜劇的成分互相摻雜，本劇上演時有多種詮釋。十八世紀的劇場，著重於喜劇層面；十九世紀時，人們開始重視浪漫的成分；到了二十世紀，本劇仍是最受歡迎的莎翁喜劇之一，常可在聖誕節見到它的蹤影。

《第十二夜》人物表

Sebastian	史裴俊	和妹妹菲兒拉是雙胞胎，兩人遭遇海難
Viola	菲兒拉	史裴俊的雙胞胎妹妹，之後男扮女裝，化名夏沙若（Cesario）
Orsino	歐析諾	一位公爵，愛慕奧莉薇
Olivia	奧莉薇	因守喪而不見男性
Antonio	安東尼	一名船長，在海難中救了史裴俊

Twelfth Night

Sebastian and his sister Viola, a young gentleman and lady of Messaline, were twins, and (which was accounted[1] a great wonder) from their birth they so much resembled each other, that, but for the difference in their dress, they could not be known apart.

They were both born in one hour, and in one hour they were both in danger of perishing[2], for they were shipwrecked[3] on the coast of Illyria, as they were making a sea-voyage together. The ship, on board of which they were, split on a rock in a violent storm, and a very small number of the ship's company escaped with their lives.

The captain of the vessel[4], with a few of the sailors that were saved, got to land in a small boat, and with them they brought Viola safe on shore, where she, poor lady, instead of rejoicing at her own deliverance[5], began to lament[6] her brother's loss; but the captain comforted her with the assurance that he had seen her brother, when the ship split, fasten himself to a strong mast[7], on which, as long as he could see anything of him for the distance, he perceived[8] him borne up above the waves.

Viola was much consoled by the hope this account gave her, and now considered how she was to dispose[9] of herself in a strange country, so far from home; and she asked the captain if he knew anything of Illyria.

"Ay, very well, madam," replied the captain, "for I was born not three hours' travel from this place."

"Who governs here?" said Viola.

The captain told her, Illyria was governed by Orsino, a duke noble in nature as well as dignity.

Viola said, she had heard her father speak of Orsino, and that he was unmarried then.

1 account [əˈkaʊnt] (v.) 認為；視為
2 perishing [ˈperiʃɪŋ] (n.) 毀滅；死亡
3 shipwreck [ˈʃɪprek] (v.) 遭遇船難
4 vessel [ˈvesəl] (n.) 船；艦
5 deliverance [dɪˈlɪvərəns] (n.) 拯救
6 lament [ləˈment] (v.) 悲傷；惋惜
7 mast [mæst] (n.) 船桅
8 perceive [pərˈsiːv] (v.) 〔正式用法〕察覺；看法
9 dispose [dɪˈspoʊz] (v.) 處理；處置

"And he is so now," said the captain; "or was so very lately, for, but a month ago, I went from here, and then it was the general talk (as you know what great ones do, the people will prattle[10] of) that Orsino sought the love of fair Olivia, a virtuous maid, the daughter of a count[11] who died twelve months ago, leaving Olivia to the protection of her brother, who shortly after died also; and for the love of this dear brother, they say, she has abjured[12] the sight and company of men."

Viola, who was herself in such a sad affliction[13] for her brother's loss, wished she could live with this lady who so tenderly mourned[14] a brother's death. She asked the captain if he could introduce her to Olivia, saying she would willingly serve this lady.

But he replied, this would be a hard thing to accomplish, because the Lady Olivia would admit no person into her house since her brother's death, not even the duke himself.

---

10 prattle ['prætl] (v.) 像小孩一樣天真地談話
11 count [kaʊnt] (n.) 伯爵
12 abjure [æb'dʒʊr] (v.) 宣布放棄 (某種信仰、權利、惡習等)
13 affliction [ə'flɪkʃən] (n.) 痛苦;苦難
14 mourn [mɔːrn] (v.) 哀悼

Then Viola formed another project in her mind, which was, in a man's habit, to serve the Duke Orsino as a page[15]. It was a strange fancy in a young lady to put on male attire[16], and pass for a boy; but the forlorn[17] and unprotected state of Viola, who was young and of uncommon beauty, alone, and in a foreign land, must plead[18] her excuse.

She having observed a fair behavior in the captain, and that he showed a friendly concern for her welfare, entrusted him with her design, and he readily engaged to assist her. Viola gave him money, and directed him to furnish her with suitable apparel[19], ordering her clothes to be made of the same color and in the same fashion her brother Sebastian used to wear, and when she was dressed in her manly garb[20], she looked so exactly like her brother that some strange errors happened by means of their being mistaken for each other; for, as will afterwards appear, Sebastian was also saved.

Viola's good friend, the captain, when he had transformed this pretty lady into a gentleman, having some interest at court, got her presented to Orsino under the feigned name of Cesario.

15 page [peɪdʒ] (n.) 僮僕
16 attire [əˈtaɪr] (n.) 〔文學用法〕〔詩的用法〕服裝
17 forlorn [fərˈlɔːrn] (a.) 〔文學用法〕〔詩的用法〕孤伶伶的
18 plead [pliːd] (v.) 以……為理由
19 apparel [əˈpærəl] (n.) 〔舊式用法〕〔文學用法〕衣服
20 garb [ɡɑːrb] (n.) 服裝（尤指某一類人所穿的服裝）

The duke was wonderfully pleased with the address and graceful deportment of this handsome youth, and made Cesario one of his pages, that being the office Viola wished to obtain: and she so well fulfilled the duties of her new station[21], and showed such a ready observance[22] and faithful attachment to her lord, that she soon became his most favored attendant.

To Cesario Orsino confided[23] the whole history of his love for the lady Olivia. To Cesario he told the long and unsuccessful suit he had made to one who, rejecting his long services, and despising his person, refused to admit him to her presence; and for the love of this lady who had so unkindly treated him, the noble Orsino, forsaking[24] the sports of the field and all manly exercises in which he used to delight, passed his hours in ignoble sloth[25], listening to the effeminate[26] sounds of soft music, gentle airs, and passionate love-songs; and neglecting the company of the wise and learned lords with whom he used to associate, he was now all day long conversing with young Cesario. Unmeet companion no doubt his grave courtiers thought Cesario was for their once noble master, the great Duke Orsino.

21 station [ˈsteɪʃən] (n.) 社會地位、身分

22 observance [əbˈzɜːrvəns] (n.) 禮儀；注意；觀察

23 confide [kənˈfaɪd] (v.) 向（某人）傾訴

24 forsake [fərˈseɪk] (v.) 放棄

25 sloth [sloʊθ] (n.) 懶散；怠惰

26 effeminate [ɪˈfemɪnət] (a.)〔貶意用法〕無男子氣概的

It is a dangerous matter for young maidens to be the confidants[27] of handsome young dukes; which Viola too soon found to her sorrow, for all that Orsino told her he endured for Olivia, she presently perceived she suffered for the love of him; and much it moved her wonder that Olivia could be so regardless of this her peerless[28] lord and master, whom she thought no one could behold without the deepest admiration, and she ventured[29] gently to hint to Orsino, that it was a pity he should affect[30] a lady who was so blind to his worthy qualities; and she said, "If a lady were to love you, my lord, as you love Olivia (and perhaps there may be one who does), if you could not love her in return) would you not tell her that you could not love, and must she not be content with this answer?"

But Orsino would not admit of this reasoning, for he denied that it was possible for any woman to love as he did. He said, no woman's heart was big enough to hold so much love, and therefore it was unfair to compare the love of any lady for him, to his love for Olivia.

27 confidant [ˈkɑːnfɪdænt] (n.) 密友；知己
28 peerless [ˈpɪrləs] (a.) 無可匹敵的
29 venture [ˈventʃər] (v.) 冒險
30 affect [əˈfekt] (v.) 喜好；愛好

Now, though Viola had the utmost deference[31] for the duke's opinions, she could not help thinking this was not quite true, for she thought her heart had full as much love in it as Orsino's had; and she said, "Ah, but I know, my lord."

"What do you know, Cesario?" said Orsino.

"Too well I know," replied Viola, "what love women may owe to men. They are as true of heart as we are. My father had a daughter loved a man, as I perhaps, were I a woman, should love your lordship."

"And what is her history?" said Orsino.

"A blank, my lord," replied Viola: "she never told her love, but let concealment[32], like a worm in the bud, feed on her damask[33] cheek. She pined[34] in thought, and with a green and yellow melancholy, she sat like Patience on a monument, smiling at Grief."

The duke inquired if this lady died of her love, but to this question Viola returned an evasive[35] answer; as probably she had feigned the story, to speak words expressive of the secret love and silent grief she suffered for Orsino.

31 deference ['defərəns] (n.) 尊敬
32 concealment [kən'siːlmənt] (n.) 隱藏
33 damask ['dæməsk] (a.) 粉紅色的
34 pine [paɪn] (v.) 消瘦；憔悴
35 evasive [ɪ'veɪsɪv] (a.) 躲避的；逃避的

While they were talking, a gentleman entered whom the duke had sent to Olivia, and he said, "So please you, my lord, I might not be admitted to the lady, but by her handmaid[36] she returned you this answer: Until seven years hence, the element itself shall not behold her face; but like a cloistress she will walk veiled, watering her chamber with her tears for the sad remembrance of her dead brother."

On hearing this, the duke exclaimed, "O she that has a heart of this fine frame, to pay this debt of love to a dead brother, how will she love, when the rich golden shaft[37] has touched her heart!" And then he said to Viola, "You know, Cesario, I have told you all the secrets of my heart; therefore, good youth, go to Olivia's house. Be not denied access; stand at her doors, and tell her, there your fixed foot shall grow till you have audience."

"And if I do speak to her, my lord, what then?" said Viola.

36 handmaid ['hændmeɪd] (n.)〔古代用法〕女僕

37 shaft [ʃæft] (n.) 箭；光線；閃光

"O then," replied Orsino, "unfold to her the passion of my love. Make a long discourse[38] to her of my dear faith. It will well become you to act my woes[39], for she will attend more to you than to one of graver aspect."

Away then went Viola; but not willingly did she undertake this courtship, for she was to woo a lady to become a wife to him she wished to marry: but having undertaken the affair, she performed it with fidelity; and Olivia soon heard that a youth was at her door who insisted upon being admitted to her presence.

"I told him," said the servant, "that you were sick: he said he knew you were, and therefore he came to speak with you. I told him that you were asleep: he seemed to have a foreknowledge of that too, and said, that therefore he must speak with you. What is to be said to him, lady? for he seems fortified against all denial, and will speak with you, whether you will or no."

---

38 discourse [dɪsˈkɔːrs] (n.) 演說
39 woe [woʊ] (n.) 悲哀；痛苦

🎧77 Olivia, curious to see who this peremptory[40] messenger might be, desired he might be admitted; and throwing her veil over her face, she said she would once more hear Orsino's embassy, not doubting but that he came from the duke, by his importunity[41].

Viola, entering, put on the most manly air she could assume[42], and affecting the fine courtier language of great men's pages, she said to the veiled lady: "Most radiant, exquisite[43], and matchless beauty, I pray you tell me if you are the lady of the house; for I should be sorry to cast away my speech upon another; for besides that it is excellently well penned[44], I have taken great pains to learn it."

"Whence come you, sir?" said Olivia.

"I can say little more than I have studied," replied Viola; and that question is out of my part."

"Are you a comedian?" said Olivia.

---

40 peremptory [pə'remptəri] (a.) 專橫的；斷然的
41 importunity [ˌɪmpɔːr'tjuːnəti] (n.) 強求
42 assume [ə'suːm] (v.) 假裝
43 exquisite [ɪk'skwɪzɪt] (a.) 優美的
44 pen [pen] (v.) 寫

78

"No," replied Viola; "and yet I am not that which I play;" meaning that she, being a woman, feigned[45] herself to be a man. And again she asked Olivia if she were the lady of the house.

Olivia said she was; and then Viola, having more curiosity to see her rival's features, than haste to deliver her master's message, said, "Good madam, let me see your face."

With this bold request Olivia was not averse[46] to comply[47]; for this haughty beauty, whom the Duke Orsino had loved so long in vain, at first sight conceived a passion for the supposed page, the humble Cesario.

When Viola asked to see her face, Olivia said, "Have you any commission[48] from your lord and master to negotiate with my face?" And then, forgetting her determination to go veiled for seven long years, she drew aside her veil, saying, "But I will draw the curtain and show the picture. Is it not well done?"

45 feign [feɪn] (v.) 假裝
46 averse [əˈvɜːrs] (a.) 反對的；嫌惡的
47 comply [kəmˈplaɪ] (v.) 順從
48 commission [kəˈmɪʃən] (n.) 委任

79

Viola replied, "It is beauty truly mixed; the red and white upon your cheeks is by Nature's own cunning hand laid on. You are the most cruel lady living, if you will lead these graces to the grave, and leave the world no copy."

"O, sir," replied Olivia, "I will not be so cruel. The world may have an inventory[49] of my beauty. As, *item*, two lips, indifferent red; *item*, two gray eyes, with lids to them; one neck; one chin; and so forth. Were you sent here to praise me?"

Viola replied, "I see what you are: you are too proud, but you are fair. My lord and master loves you. O such a love could but be recompensed[50], though you were crowned the queen of beauty: for Orsino loves you with adoration and with tears, with groans that thunder love, and sighs of fire."

"Your lord," said Olivia, "knows well my mind. I cannot love him; yet I doubt not he is virtuous; I know him to be noble and of high estate, of fresh and spotless youth. All voices proclaim[51] him learned, courteous, and valiant[52]; yet I cannot love him, he might have taken his answer long ago."

49 inventory [ˈɪnvəntɔːri] (n.) 清單

50 recompense [ˈrekəmpens] (v.) 報償

51 proclaim [prouˈkleɪm] (v.) 宣告；聲明

52 valiant [ˈvæliənt] (a.) 勇敢的

"If I did love you as my master does," said Viola, "I would make me a willow cabin at your gates, and call upon your name, I would write complaining sonnets on Olivia, and sing them in the dead of the night: your name should sound among the hills, and I would make Echo, the babbling[53] gossip of the air, cry out *Olivia*. O you should not rest between the elements of earth and air, but you should pity me."

"You might do much," said Olivia: "what is your parentage?'"

Viola replied, "Above my fortunes, yet my state is well. I am a gentleman."

Olivia now reluctantly dismissed Viola, saying: "Go to your master, and tell him, I cannot love him. Let him send no more, unless perchance[54] you come again to tell me how he takes it."

And Viola departed, bidding the lady farewell by the name of Fair Cruelty.

When she was gone, Olivia repeated the words, *Above my fortunes, yet my state is well. I am a gentleman.* And she said aloud, "I will be sworn he is; his tongue, his face, his limbs, action, and spirit, plainly show he is a gentleman."

53 babbling ['bæblɪŋ] (a.) 多嘴的
54 perchance [pər'tʃæns] (adv.) 或許；可能

And then she wished Cesario was the duke; and perceiving the fast hold he had taken on her affections, she blamed herself for her sudden love: but the gentle blame which people lay upon their own faults has no deep root; and presently the noble Lady Olivia so far forgot the inequality between her fortunes and those of this seeming page, as well as the maidenly reserve[55] which is the chief ornament of a lady's character, that she resolved to court the love of young Cesario, and sent a servant after him with a diamond ring, under the pretense that he had left it with her as a present from Orsino.

She hoped by thus artfully making Cesario a present of the ring, she should give him some intimation[56] of her design; and truly it did make Viola suspect; for knowing that Orsino had sent no ring by her, she began to recollect[57] that Olivia's looks and manner were expressive of admiration, and she presently guessed her master's mistress had fallen in love with her.

"Alas!" said she, "the poor lady might as well love a dream. Disguise[58] I see is wicked, for it has caused Olivia to breathe as fruitless sighs for me as I do for Orsino."

Viola returned to Orsino's palace, and related[59] to her lord the ill success of the negotiation, repeating the command of Olivia, that the duke should trouble her no more.

Yet still the duke persisted in hoping that the gentle Cesario would in time be able to persuade her to show some pity, and therefore he bade him he should go to her again the next day. In the meantime, to pass away the tedious[60] interval, he commanded a song which he loved to be sung; and he said, "My good Cesario, when I heard that song last night, methought it did relieve my passion much. Mark it, Cesario, it is old and plain. The spinsters and the knitters when they sit in the sun, and the young maids that weave their thread with bone, chant this song. It is silly, yet I love it, for it tells of the innocence of love in the old times."

55 reserve [rɪ'zɜːrv] (n.) 自制；含蓄
56 intimation [ˌɪntɪ'meɪʃən] (n.) 提示；暗示
57 recollect [ˌrekə'lekt] (v.) 憶起
58 disguise [dɪs'gaɪz] (n.) (v.) 喬裝
59 relate [rɪ'leɪt] (v.) 講述
60 tedious ['tiːdɪəs] (a.) 沈悶的

82

Song

Come away, come away, Death,
And in sad cypress[61] let me be laid;
Fly away, fly away, breath,
I am slain by a fair cruel maid.
My shroud[62] of white stuck all with yew[63], O prepare it!
My part of death no one so true did share it.
Not a flower, not a flower sweet,
On my black coffin let there be strewn[64]:
Not a friend, not a friend greet
My poor corpse, where my bones shall be thrown.
A thousand thousand sighs to save, lay me O where
Sad true lover never find my grave, to weep there!

Viola did not fail to mark the words of the old song, which in such true simplicity described the pangs[65] of unrequited[66] love, and she bore testimony[67] in her countenance[68] of feeling what the song expressed. Her sad looks were observed by Orsino, who said to her, "My life upon it, Cesario, though you are so young, your eye has looked upon some face that it loves: has it not, boy?"

61 cypress ['saɪprəs] (n.) 柏樹

62 shroud [ʃraʊd] (n.) 壽衣

63 yew [juː] (n.)〔植〕紫杉

64 strew [struː] (v.) 撒；使散落

65 pang [pæŋ] (n.) 劇痛

66 unrequited [ˌʌnrɪˈkwaɪtɪd] (a.) 無報酬的

67 testimony ['testɪmoʊni] (n.) 宣言；陳述

68 countenance ['kaʊntɪnəns] (n.) 面容

83

"A little, with your leave," replied Viola.

"And what kind of woman, and of what age is she?" said Orsino.

"Of your age and of your complexion[69], my lord," said Viola; which made the duke smile to hear this fair young boy loved a woman so much older than himself, and of a man's dark complexion; but Viola secretly meant Orsino, and not a woman like him.

When Viola made her second visit to Olivia, she found no difficulty in gaining access to her. Servants soon discover when their ladies delight to converse with handsome young messengers; and the instant Viola arrived the gates were thrown wide open, and the duke's page was shown into Olivia's apartment with great respect; and when Viola told Olivia that she was come once more to plead in her lord's behalf, this lady said, "I desired you never to speak of him again; but if you would undertake another suit, I had rather hear you solicit[70], than music from the spheres."

---

69 complexion [kəmˈplekʃən] (n.) 膚色；面貌
70 solicit [səˈlɪsɪt] (v.) 懇求

84

This was pretty plain speaking, but Olivia soon explained herself still more plainly, and openly confessed her love; and when she saw displeasure with perplexity[71] expressed in Viola's face, she said, "O what a deal of scorn looks beautiful in the contempt and anger of his lip! Cesario, by the roses of the spring, by maidhood, honor, and by truth, I love you so, that, in spite of your pride, I have neither wit nor reason to conceal my passion."

But in vain the lady wooed; Viola hastened from her presence, threatening never more to come to plead Orsino's love; and all the reply she made to Olivia's fond solicitation was, a declaration of a resolution *Never to love any woman.*

No sooner had Viola left the lady than a claim was made upon her valor[72]. A gentleman, a rejected suitor of Olivia, who had learned how that lady had favored the duke's messenger, challenged him to fight a duel. What should poor Viola do, who, though she carried a man-like outside, had a true woman's heart, and feared to look on her own sword?

---

71 perplexity [pərˈplɛksəti] (n.) 困惑
72 valor [ˈvælər] (n.) 勇敢
73 formidable [ˈfɔːrmɪdəbəl] (a.) 令人畏懼的

When she saw her formidable[73] rival advancing towards her with his sword drawn, she began to think of confessing that she was a woman; but she was relieved at once from her terror, and the shame of such a discovery, by a stranger that was passing by, who made up to them, and as if he had been long known to her, and were her dearest friend, said to her opponent, "If this young gentleman has done offense[74], I will take the fault on me; and if you offend him, I will for his sake defy[75] you."

Before Viola had time to thank him for his protection, or to inquire the reason of his kind interference, her new friend met with an enemy where his bravery was of no use to him; for the officers of justice coming up in that instant, apprehended[76] the stranger in the duke's name, to answer for an offense he had committed some years before: and he said to Viola, "This comes with seeking you:" and then he asked her for a purse, saying: "Now my necessity makes me ask for my purse, and it grieves me much more for what I cannot do for you, than for what befalls myself. You stand amazed, but be of comfort."

74 offense [ə'fens] (n.) 觸怒
75 defy [dɪ'faɪ] (v.) 公然反抗
76 apprehend [ˌæprɪ'hend] (v.) 逮捕

His words did indeed amaze Viola, and she protested she knew him not, nor had ever received a purse from him; but for the kindness he had just shown her, she offered him a small sum of money, being nearly the whole she possessed.

And now the stranger spoke severe things, charging her with ingratitude[77] and unkindness. He said, "This youth, whom you see here, I snatched from the jaws of death, and for his sake alone I came to Illyria, and have fallen into this danger."

But the officers cared little for hearkening[78] to the complaints of their prisoner, and they hurried him off, saying, "What is that to us?"

And as he was carried away, he called Viola by the name of Sebastian, reproaching[79] the supposed Sebastian for disowning[80] his friend, as long as he was within hearing.

---

77 ingratitude [ɪnˈgrætɪtuːd] (n.) 忘恩負義
78 hearken [ˈhɑːrkən] (v.) 傾聽（與 to 連用）
79 reproach [rɪˈproutʃ] (v.) 責備
80 disown [dɪsˈoun] (v.) 否認

When Viola heard herself called Sebastian, though the stranger was taken away too hastily for her to ask an explanation, she conjectured[81] that this seeming mystery might arise from her being mistaken for her brother; and she began to cherish hopes that it was her brother whose life this man said he had preserved.

And so indeed it was. The stranger whose name was Antonio, was a sea-captain. He had taken Sebastian up into his ship, when, almost exhausted with fatigue, he was floating on the mast to which he had fastened himself in the storm.

Antonio conceived such a friendship for Sebastian, that he resolved to accompany him whithersoever he went; and when the youth expressed a curiosity to visit Orsino's court, Antonio, rather than part from him, came to Illyria, though he knew, if his person should be known there, his life would be in danger, because in a sea-fight he had once dangerously wounded the Duke Orsino's nephew. This was the offense for which he was now made a prisoner.

Antonio and Sebastian had landed together but a few hours before Antonio met Viola. He had given his purse to Sebastian, desiring him to use it freely if he saw anything he wished to purchase, telling him he would wait at the inn, while Sebastian went to view the town; but Sebastian not returning at the time appointed, Antonio had ventured out to look for him, and Viola being dressed the same, and in face so exactly resembling her brother, Antonio drew his sword (as he thought) in defense of the youth he had saved, and when Sebastian (as he supposed) disowned him, and denied him his own purse, no wonder he accused him of ingratitude.

Viola, when Antonio was gone, fearing a second invitation to fight, slunk[82] home as fast as she could. She had not been long gone, when her adversary[83] thought he saw her return; but it was her brother Sebastian, who happened to arrive at this place, and he said, "Now, sir, have I met with you again? There's for you"; and struck him a blow.

---

81 conjecture [kən'dʒektʃər] (v.) 推測；猜測
82 slunk [slʌŋk] (v.) 潛逃；溜走
83 adversary ['ædvərseri] (n.) 敵手；對手

Sebastian was no coward; he returned the blow with interest, and drew his sword.

A lady now put a stop to this duel, for Olivia came out of the house, and she too mistaking Sebastian for Cesario, invited him to come into her house, expressing much sorrow at the rude attack he had met with. Though Sebastian was as much surprised at the courtesy of this lady as at the rudeness of his unknown foe, yet he went very willingly into the house, and Olivia was delighted to find Cesario (as she thought him) become more sensible of her attentions; for though their features were exactly the same, there was none of the contempt and anger to be seen in his face, which she had complained of when she told her love to Cesario.

Sebastian did not at all object to the fondness the lady lavished[84] on him. He seemed to take it in very good part, yet he wondered how it had come to pass, and he was rather inclined to think Olivia was not in her right senses; but perceiving that she was mistress of a fine house, and that she ordered her affairs and seemed to govern her family discreetly[85], and that in all but her sudden love for him she appeared in

the full possession of her reason, he well approved of the courtship; and Olivia finding Cesario in this good humor, and fearing he might change his mind, proposed that, as she had a priest in the house, they should be instantly married.

84 lavish [ˈlævɪʃ] (v.) 揮霍；濫施
85 discreetly [dɪˈskriːtli] (adv.) 謹慎地

Sebastian assented to this proposal; and when the marriage ceremony was over, he left his lady for a short time, intending to go and tell his friend Antonio the good fortune that he had met with.

In the meantime Orsino came to visit Olivia: and at the moment he arrived before Olivia's house, the officers of justice brought their prisoner, Antonio, before the duke. Viola was with Orsino, her master; and when Antonio saw Viola, whom he still imagined to be Sebastian, he told the duke in what manner he had rescued this youth from the perils[86] of the sea; and after fully relating all the kindness he had really shown to Sebastian, he ended his complaint with saying, that for three months, both day and night, this ungrateful youth had been with him.

But now the lady Olivia coming forth from her house, the duke could no longer attend to Antonio's story; and he said, "Here comes the countess: now heaven walks on earth! but for thee, fellow, thy[87] words are madness. Three months has this youth attended[88] on me": and then he ordered Antonio to be taken aside.

---

86 peril ['perəl] (n.) 危險的事物
87 thy [ðaɪ] (pron.) 〔古代用法〕你的（thou 的所有格）
88 attend [ə'tend] (v.) 侍候；看護

But Orsino's heavenly countess soon gave the duke cause to accuse Cesario as much of ingratitude as Antonio had done, for all the words he could hear Olivia speak were words of kindness to Cesario: and when he found his page had obtained this high place in Olivia's favor, he threatened him with all the terrors of his just revenge: and as he was going to depart, he called Viola to follow him, saying: "Come, boy, with me. My thoughts are ripe for mischief."

Though it seemed in his jealous rage he was going to doom Viola to instant death, yet her love made her no longer a coward, and she said she would most joyfully suffer death to give her master ease.

But Olivia would not so lose her husband, and she cried, "Where goes my Cesario?"

Viola replied, "After him I love more than my life."

Olivia, however, prevented their departure by loudly proclaiming that Cesario was her husband, and sent for the priest, who declared that not two hours had passed since he had married the lady Olivia to this

young man. In vain Viola protested she was not
married to Olivia; the evidence of that lady and the
priest made Orsino believe that his page had robbed
him of the treasure he prized above his life.

90

But thinking that it was past recall, he was bidding farewell to his faithless mistress, and the *young dissembler*[89], her husband, as he called Viola, warning her never to come in his sight again, when (as it seemed to them) a miracle appeared! for another Cesario entered, and addressed Olivia as his wife.

This new Cesario was Sebastian, the real husband of Olivia; and when their wonder had a little ceased at seeing two persons with the same face, the same voice, and the same habit, the brother and sister began to question each other; for Viola could scarce be persuaded that her brother was living, and Sebastian knew not how to account for the sister he supposed drowned being found in the habit of a young man. But Viola presently acknowledged that she was indeed Viola, and his sister, under that disguise.

When all the errors were cleared up which the extreme likeness between this twin brother and sister had occasioned[90], they laughed at the Lady Olivia for the pleasant mistake she had made in falling in love with a woman; and Olivia showed no dislike to her exchange, when she found she had wedded the brother instead of the sister.

89 dissembler [dɪˈsemblər] (n.) 偽君子
90 occasion [əˈkeɪʒən] (v.) 引起；惹起

91

The hopes of Orsino were for ever at an end by this marriage of Olivia, and with his hopes, all his fruitless love seemed to vanish away, and all his thoughts were fixed on the event of his favorite, young Cesario, being changed into a fair lady.

He viewed Viola with great attention, and he remembered how very handsome he had always thought Cesario was, and he concluded she would look very beautiful in a woman's attire; and then he remembered how often she had said *she loved him*, which at the time seemed only the dutiful expressions of a faithful page; but now he guessed that something more was meant, for many of her pretty sayings, which were like riddles to him, came now into his mind, and he no sooner remembered all these things than he resolved to make Viola his wife; and he said to her (he still could not help calling her Cesario and boy): "Boy, you have said to me a thousand times that you should never love a woman like to me, and for the faithful service you have done for me so much beneath your soft and tender breeding, and since you have called me master so long, you shall now be your master's mistress, and Orsino's true duchess."

Olivia, perceiving Orsino was making over that heart, which she had so ungraciously rejected, to Viola, invited them to enter her house, and offered the assistance of the good priest, who had married her to Sebastian in the morning, to perform the same ceremony in the remaining part of the day for Orsino and Viola.

Thus the twin brother and sister were both wedded on the same day: the storm and shipwreck, which had separated them, being the means of bringing to pass their high and mighty fortunes. Viola was the wife of Orsino, the duke of Illyria, and Sebastian the husband of the rich and noble countess, the Lady Olivia.

《第十二夜》名句選

Duke Orsino   If music be the food of love, play on,
Give me excess of it: that surfeiting,
The appetite may sicken, and so die.
(I, i, 1–3)

歐析諾公爵   音樂若是愛情的食糧，就演奏下去吧，
給我過量的音樂，讓我飲食過度，
讓食慾失衡，因此而死。

（第一幕，第一景，1–3 行）

Duke Orsino	And what's her history?
Viola	A blank, my lord. She never told her love,
	But let concealment, like a worm i' th' bud,
	Feed on her damask cheek. She pined in
	thought:
	And, with a green and yellow melancholy,
	She sat like Patience on a monument,
	Smiling at Grief.

(II, Iv, 110–116)

歐析諾公爵	那她的戀愛過程呢？
菲兒拉	一片空白，殿下。她從不透露自己的感情，
	而是將它隱藏起來，就像花苞裡的小蟲，
	侵蝕她的緋頰。她因相思而憔悴，
	帶著綠黃色調的憂鬱，
	她如「耐性」，坐在碑上，
	對著「憂傷」微笑。

（第二幕，第四景，110-116 行）

仲夏夜之夢

P. 26 　　雅典城有一條法律，認可人民有權強迫女兒遵從父母所安排的婚姻，如果女兒不肯聽從父命，父親可以依法請求處死女兒。但做父親的畢竟不希望女兒去送死，因此就算做女兒的不太聽話，也極少有人會訴諸這條法律，做父母的有時只是會拿來嚇唬城裡的姑娘們。

　　話說有一回，有位叫做伊吉斯的老翁，竟真的為此跑來找底修斯（當時管轄雅典的公爵）。他控訴女兒荷米雅，說他已經把她許配給德米崔斯，對方是個出身雅典貴族家庭的年輕人，

BVT·I·WILL·WED·THEE·IN ANOTHER·KEY ACT·1·SCENE·1·

荷米雅卻拒絕這門婚事，說她愛的是一名叫萊桑德的雅典青年。伊吉斯遂要求底修斯主持公道，要求訴諸這條峻法來處治女兒。

P. 27 　　荷米雅辯解說，她之所以違抗父命，是因為德米崔斯之前就追求過她的好友海蓮娜，況且海蓮娜也瘋狂迷戀德米崔斯。她理由充分，解釋不從父命的原因，但嚴苛的伊吉斯不為所動。

　　底修斯君主偉大而仁慈，但怎奈他也無權變更國家的法律。他能做的只是給荷米雅四天的時

間考慮，四天後若仍不肯嫁給德米崔斯，那只好依法處斬。

P. 29 　公爵退庭之後，荷米雅前去找情人萊桑德，跟他說明自己的困境，表示她不是放棄他去嫁給德米崔斯，就是只能再活四天。

　　這個壞消息讓萊桑德痛苦萬分。這時他想起，他有個姑媽住在雅典城外，離雅典有段距離，那條峻法在那裡不具效力（這條法律無法擴及雅典城外）。於是他向荷米雅提議當晚就離家出走，跟他一起到姑媽家，然後在那裡結婚。

　　「我在城外幾里遠的林子裡等你。就是那個令人心曠神怡的林子，我們常在宜人的五月和海蓮娜去那裡散步。」萊桑德說。

P. 31 　荷米雅欣然贊成。她沒有跟任何人透露這個逃亡計畫，除了好友海蓮娜。未料海蓮娜因為私心（姑娘們會為愛做傻事），決定去跟德米崔斯通報這件事情。她並不指望洩漏好友的秘密會有好處，只不過是想跟著她不忠的情人到林子裡去，因為她知道德米崔斯一定會去林子裡找荷米雅。

　　萊桑德和荷米雅相約會面的林子，是人稱「精靈」的那些小東西最喜歡出沒的地方。

　　精靈國的仙王歐伯龍和仙后泰坦妮，他們會帶著所有的小

隨從，在林子裡舉行午夜
歡宴。

P. 32　　這時，小仙王和小仙
后又吵了起來。在這心曠
神怡的林子裡，當他們在
月下的樹蔭中漫步時，總
是一碰面就拌嘴，吵得所
有精靈都嚇得爬進橡實殼
裡躲起來。

　　他們這次吵架的原
因，是因為泰坦妮不肯把
她調包偷來的小男孩交給
歐伯龍。小男孩的母親是泰坦妮的好友，男孩的母親死後，仙
后就從奶媽那裡偷走男孩，帶回林子裡撫養。

　　今晚，情人們打算在林子裡碰面。當時泰坦妮正帶著幾名
宮女散步，碰巧遇見也有朝臣伴行的歐伯龍。

　　「自命不凡的泰坦妮，這月光下還真是冤家路窄！」仙王說。

　　仙后回答道：「什麼？醋罈子歐伯龍，是你啊？仙子們，
我和他誓不兩立，咱們走另一條路。」

P. 34　　歐伯龍說：「等等，你這個魯莽的仙子！我不是你的主子
嗎？怎麼泰坦妮跟她的歐伯龍作起對來了？把你偷來的男孩給
我做僮僕。」

　　「你死了這條心吧！」仙后回答：「就算你拿整個仙國來跟
我換，我也不會給你的。」說完她便氣沖沖地離開。

　　歐伯龍說：「隨便你！你這樣對我，我要你今晚就有得
受。」

歐伯龍把他最寵信的幕僚帕克給差來。帕克（有時被稱為「好傢伙羅賓」）是個精明狡猾的精靈，常在附近的村子裡搗蛋尋開心。他有時會跑去製酪場把乳脂刮走，有時會把自己的小巧身體塞進攪乳器裡，在裡面大跳熱舞，如此一來，別說製酪姑娘無法把乳汁攪成奶油，就算是換作村裡的壯丁，也會白費力氣。如果帕克是在釀酒鍋裡作怪，啤酒也會遭殃。

Oberon and Puck

P. 36

幾個好鄰居齊聚喝些好酒時，帕克會變成烤野蘋果，跳進酒杯裡，趁老太婆準備喝下時，在她的唇間彈上跳下，潑得她乾癟癟的下巴滿是酒。又當老太婆煞有其事地準備坐下，跟街坊說說悲傷的故事時，帕克就把她屁股下的三腳凳給抽走，讓可憐的老太婆摔個正著，讓那些老長舌們見了捧腹大笑，還發誓說從來也沒這麼開心過。

「帕克，你過來！」歐伯龍對這個快活的夜遊小仙子說：「你去把姑娘們說的什麼『空戀花』拿來。只要把這種紫色小花的汁液，滴在睡著的人的眼皮上，當人醒來後，就會愛上最先映入眼簾的東西。我要趁泰坦妮睡著後，把花汁滴在她的眼皮上，那她醒來後就會對最先看到的東西一見鐘情，管那東西是獅子、熊、愛搗蛋的猴子，還是瞎攪和的猩猩。我是有另一種可以解除法力的法術，不過她得先把男孩送給我當僮僕。」

P. 37　　　主子的鬼把戲讓愛胡鬧的帕克很亢奮,帕克立刻遵照命令。在等帕克回來的空檔,歐伯龍看到德米崔斯和海蓮娜走進林子,無意中聽到德米崔斯罵海蓮娜是跟屁蟲,很不客氣地奚落她,但海蓮娜仍然語氣溫婉,要他回想自己曾經如何愛過她,如何真情告白過,而今卻扔下她(如他自己所說的),也不管她會不會碰到野獸,她只好緊追在後。

P. 38　　　仙王一向對忠貞的情人特別有好感,所以很同情海蓮娜。萊桑德說過,他們以前常在這個令人心曠神怡的林子裡月下漫步,那麼在海蓮娜還有德米崔斯憐惜的那段快樂日子裡,也許歐伯龍就曾見過她。

　　　這時帕克帶回了紫色小花,歐伯龍對這個寵臣說:「這花你拿一點去。那裡有個可愛的雅典姑娘,她愛上一個傲慢的小伙子。你要是看到小伙子在睡覺,就滴幾滴情水在他眼睛上,不過你要等姑娘在他附近時才滴,讓他醒來後最先映入眼裡的,是這一位他看不上眼的姑娘。你只要看誰穿著雅典的衣服,就知道是那個小伙子了。」

P. 39　　帕克說這件事包在他身上沒問題。歐伯龍離開後就溜進泰坦妮的臥房，當時泰坦妮正準備就寢。她的仙居臥房是一座花壇，長滿野生百里香、野櫻草和芬芳的紫羅蘭，架著野忍冬、麝香玫瑰、野薔薇搭蓋成的篷頂。泰坦妮每晚都會在這裡休息，用釉亮的蛇皮當被子。蛇皮很小一片，但足以裹住仙子。

P. 40　　歐伯龍看到泰坦妮正下令給仙子，囑咐在她睡覺時仙子們該執行的任務。仙后說：「你們有些要去撲滅麝香玫瑰花苞裡的病蟲；有些要去征伐蝙蝠，討些皮翅膀回來給我的小精靈做外套；有些要去監視每到夜晚就吵吵鬧鬧的貓頭鷹，不要讓牠靠近我。不過，現在首先要做的就是唱歌哄我睡覺！」

　　於是他們開始歌唱——

雙舌花蛇和刺蝟，
不要讓人來瞧見；
蝾螈水蜥莫搗蛋，
要離仙后遠一點。
夜鷹旋律伴我們，
同唱甜蜜催眠曲：
睡吧睡吧快睡吧；
睡吧睡吧快睡吧；
災害魔法和符籙，
不能侵害美仙后；
催眠曲中道晚安。

P. 42　　仙子唱完動聽安眠曲哄仙后入睡後，紛紛離去，去執行重要任務。歐伯龍見狀，便悄悄挨近泰坦妮，在她的眼皮上滴上情水，說道——

醒來所見，
即為至愛。

　　再說荷米雅。她不肯嫁給德米崔斯，為躲避死罪，當天半夜便離家出走。她一走進林子，就看到親愛的萊桑德在等她，準備帶她到姑媽家。荷米雅走得筋疲力竭，在穿越林子不到一半的路程時，細心呵護這位可愛姑娘的萊桑德，要她先在堤道的柔軟青苔上休息，等天亮再啟程。荷米雅為了他，可是連性命都不顧了。萊桑德躺在離她不遠的地方，兩人旋即入睡。

P. 44　　這時帕克出現，他看到熟睡的美少年穿著雅典衣服，旁邊躺著一位俏姑娘，就以為他們一定是歐伯龍要他找的雅典姑娘和傲慢情人。既然現在只有這兩個人，帕克心想，男子醒來後最先看到的當然是那位女子，於是動手就往男子的眼裡滴下紫色小花的花汁。

　　未料海蓮娜竟在此時出現，結果萊桑德醒後看到的不是荷米雅，而是海蓮娜。說來真不可思議，情水的魔法威力很大，讓萊桑德頓時愛上海蓮娜，忘記了荷米雅。

　　要是萊桑德醒後最先看到的是荷米雅，帕克的粗心大意就無傷大雅子，因為萊桑德本來就對那位忠貞的姑娘很痴情了。

　　可是現在，情水硬是讓可憐的萊桑德忘記真愛荷米雅。他移情別戀，留荷米雅半夜獨自一人睡在林子裡，這真是個不幸的意外。

P. 46　　因此不幸的事情就這樣發生了。前面說過，德米崔斯想甩開海蓮娜，海蓮娜一路在後面追，但長距離跑起來，男子的腳力比較好，海蓮娜沒多久就跟丟了。她找不到德米崔斯，心情很沮喪，孤伶伶地四處徘徊，後來就走到了萊桑德睡覺的地方。

「啊！躺在地上的是萊桑德，他是死了還是睡著了？」海蓮娜伸手摸摸他，說道：「先生啊，如果你還活著，就醒醒吧！」

萊桑德聽到這話便張開眼睛（情水即刻生效），立刻狂熱地對她傾訴衷心，說她貌美遠勝荷米雅，好比白鴿遠勝烏鴉，還說了一些他願意為美麗的她赴湯蹈火之類的痴心話。

P. 48　海蓮娜知道萊桑德是好友荷米雅的情人，也知道他真心要娶她為妻，所以聽到他講這些話，她非常生氣（這也怪不得她），認為萊桑德在愚弄她。

她說：「啊！我為什麼生來就要被人人欺負嘲笑呢？小伙子，德米崔斯從來不給我好臉色，也不對我說好聽的話，難道這還不夠嗎？不夠嗎？你竟然還要這樣調戲我？萊桑德，我還以為你是正人君子！」

她氣呼呼地說完後跑開，萊桑德見狀追了上去，把正在睡夢中的荷米雅忘得一乾二淨。

荷米雅醒來後，發現周圍只有自己一個人，不禁難過又害怕。她在林子裡踱步，不曉得萊桑德怎麼樣了，也不知道要去哪裡找他。

P. 49　這時，歐伯龍找到了德米崔斯。德米崔斯要找荷米雅和情

255

敵萊桑德找不到，累得睡了過去。歐伯龍問過帕克，知道情水滴錯了人。現在既然看到了要找的人，歐伯龍就用情水滴在德米崔斯熟睡的眼皮上。德米崔斯旋即醒來，他一醒來就看到海蓮娜。他和萊桑德一樣，對她展開瘋狂的追求。萊桑德隨後出現，後面還跟著荷米雅（帕克不幸的過失，讓荷米雅現在只好追著情人跑）。萊桑德和德米崔斯兩人就在同一種咒水的驅使下，一齊追求海蓮娜。

P. 50　　海蓮娜很吃驚，以為德米崔斯、萊桑德和昔日好友荷米雅串通好要來捉弄她。

　　荷米雅也和海蓮娜一樣吃驚，因為本來都喜歡她的萊桑德和德米崔斯，現在卻都成了海蓮娜的情人，而且看起來不像是在惡作劇。

　　這兩位曾經是密友的姑娘，不禁怒言相向。

　　「狠心的荷米雅，你叫萊桑德用虛偽的甜言蜜語來氣我，你的另一個情人德米崔斯視我如敝屣，你現在也要他捧我是女神、仙女、絕色、寶貝、天人？他討厭我，要不是你唆使他來嘲弄我，他才不會跟我說這些話。狠心的荷米雅啊，你竟然和男人聯合起來欺負你可憐的朋友，你忘了我們同窗的情誼了嗎？荷米雅呀，有多少次我們同坐在一張椅墊，唱著同一首歌，一起繡著同一朵花，描著同一個圖樣。我們就像並蒂櫻桃，一起長大，永不分開！荷米雅，你和男人聯合起來欺負你可憐的朋友，你這樣不是不顧交情、有失身分嗎？」海蓮娜說。

P. 51　　「你說得這麼激動我才莫名其妙呢！我沒有愚弄你，是你在愚弄我吧！」荷米雅回答。

　　「唉，你們就繼續這樣假惺惺地裝下去吧，等我轉過身，你們就對我做鬼臉，互相使眼色，繼續戲弄我。要是你們還有點同情心或是風度，還懂得一點禮節，你們就不會這樣對我了。」海蓮娜說。

在海蓮娜和荷米雅吵架時，德米崔斯和萊桑德轉身離開，準備到林子裡去為海蓮娜決鬥。

兩位姑娘一發現德米崔斯和萊桑不見了，隨即分道揚鑣，再度在林子裡苦苦尋覓各自的情人。

P. 52　仙王和小帕克在一旁聽她們鬥嘴，等她們一離開，仙王就對帕克說：「帕克，你是不小心的，還是故意的？」

「精靈之王，你要相信我，我真是弄錯了。您不是要我去認穿雅典衣服的人嗎？不過話說回來，事情演變成這樣，也沒什麼大不了的，他們這樣吵吵鬧鬧，也滿有趣的。」帕克答道。

P. 53　歐伯龍說：「你也聽到了德米崔斯和萊桑德要去找地方決鬥，我要你讓今晚起濃霧，教這些吵鬧的情人在黑夜裡迷路，讓他們誰也找不到誰。你裝他們每個人的聲音，去跟每個人講話，用話激他們，讓他們以為是情敵在講話，引誘他們跟你走，讓他們累到走不動為止。等他們都睡著了，就把這個花汁滴進萊桑德的眼裡，他醒來就會忘記新歡海蓮娜，心又回到荷米雅的身上。這樣一來，這兩位美姑娘就能快快樂樂地跟各自所愛的男人在一起了。他們會把這一切當作是一場惱人的夢罷了。快去吧，帕克，我

要去看我的泰坦妮愛上了誰。」

P. 55　　泰坦妮在睡夢中，歐伯龍看到附近來了個鄉巴佬。鄉巴佬在林子裡迷了路，正在休憩。歐伯龍說：「這個傢伙會成為我那泰坦妮的真愛。」說完就拿了個驢頭套在鄉巴佬的頭上，驢頭的大小這麼剛好，看起來簡直就像原本就長在他身上一樣。

歐伯龍小心翼翼地把驢頭套在他頭上，不過還是吵醒了他。他站起來，不知道歐伯龍對他動了什麼手腳，直往仙后睡覺的寢宮走去。

「啊！竟有這般的天使？」泰坦妮睜開眼睛，紫色小花的花汁開始產生效力。她說：「你的智慧和你的美貌一樣超凡嗎？」

「唉，這位太太呀！」傻呼呼的鄉巴佬說：「我要是夠機伶，找得到路走出這林子，我就心滿意足了。」

「不要離開林子！」深情款款的皇后說：「我可不是普通的精靈。我愛你，你跟我走，我會派仙子侍候你。」

P. 57　　她叫來了四個仙子，分別是豌豆花、蜘蛛網、飛天蛾和芥末子。

皇后說：「你們好好侍候這個迷人的先生。跟隨他的步伐飛舞，在他面前嬉戲，餵他吃葡萄和杏果，偷蜜蜂的蜂蜜來送給他。」她對鄉巴佬說：「你過來，跟我坐在一起。我俊俏的驢，讓我摸摸你毛茸茸的可愛臉蛋吧！我要吻吻你漂亮的大

耳朵，我的溫柔寶貝兒！」

「豌豆花呢？」驢頭鄉巴佬問。他不太理會仙后的追求，倒是很得意自己新有的侍從。

「我在這裡，先生。」小豌豆花回答。

「幫我搔搔頭。」鄉巴佬又問：「蜘蛛網呢？」

「是，先生。」蜘蛛網回答。

P. 58　　蠢鄉巴佬說：「蜘蛛網好先生，幫我把薊頂上那隻紅色小蜜蜂弄死，再把那個蜜囊拿過來。不要慌慌張張，小心別打破蜜囊，蜘蛛網先生，要是你沾了滿身的蜜，我會很過意不去。芥末子呢？」

「是，先生。您有何吩咐？」芥末子回答。

鄉巴佬說：「沒事。好芥末子先生，你就和豌豆花先生幫我搔癢。我該去剃頭了，我老覺得我臉上的毛好像太多了。」

「親愛的，你想吃點什麼？我有個冒險犯難的精靈，他可以找到松鼠的儲糧，給你拿些新鮮的核桃來。」皇后說。

「我比較想吃一大把豌豆乾。」鄉巴佬戴了驢頭之後，胃口也變得跟驢子一樣，他說：「也請你叫你那些人不要來吵我，我要睡覺了。」

P. 61　　「那你就睡吧，我會把你抱在我的懷裡睡覺。啊，我是如此愛你！如此寵你啊！」皇后說。

看到鄉巴佬睡在皇后的懷裡，仙王走到她面前，指責她竟然這樣把感情放在一頭驢子的身上。

她無法否認，鄉巴佬就睡在她懷裡，她還在驢頭上插了圈花朵。

歐伯龍嘲笑她一番後，又跟她要那個偷來的男孩。被丈夫看到自己和新歡在一起，她羞愧得難以拒絕他的要求。

就這樣，歐伯龍得到了巴望已久的小男孩來做他的僮僕，但他卻開始同情起泰坦妮，因為自己的惡作劇，才讓她見不得人。於是他就把解藥花汁滴在她眼裡，她隨即清醒。她不明白自己剛剛才為何會意亂情迷，她現在改口說，她看到這個畸形怪物就討厭。

P.62　歐伯龍把鄉巴佬頭上的驢頭取下，讓他頂著自己的那顆蠢腦袋繼續睡覺。

現在，歐伯龍和泰坦妮言歸於好，他就把那些情人的故事和半夜吵架的經過都告訴她，泰坦妮好奇的也想跟去看看結局。

仙王和仙后找到兩位男子和他們的美麗姑娘，他們就睡在草地上，彼此相距不遠。帕克為了彌補過錯，想辦法把他們引到同一個地方，而不讓彼此發現到對方，然後再用仙王給他的解藥，小心翼翼解除了萊桑德眼裡的魔咒。

荷米雅最先醒來，她看

到狠心離去的萊桑德就睡在附近。她看著他，不明白發生什麼事了。此時萊桑德也睜開眼睛，一眼就看到他親愛的荷米雅。他從魔法中清醒過來，恢復了理智和對荷米雅的愛。他們談起當晚的奇遇，搞不清楚事情是真的發生過，還是兩人做了一場相同而離奇的夢。

P. 64 海蓮娜和德米崔斯這時也醒了過來。睡了一場好覺之後，海蓮娜不再煩躁生氣，現在又聽到德米崔斯對她告白，心裡很開心。尤其看出他的告白都是真心話之後，她更是驚訝興奮。

這兩位夜遊的美麗姑娘現在不再是情敵，兩人重修舊好，釋懷了曾經脫口而出的惡言。她們心平氣和地討論接下來應該要怎麼做。不久，他們都同意，既然德米崔斯不再想娶荷米雅，那他就應該勸她父親撤銷無情的死刑。為此，德米崔斯準備返回雅典，結果遇到了荷米雅的父親伊吉斯也來到了林子，想找尋逃家的女兒。

伊吉斯得知德米崔斯不會娶他的女兒後，便不再反對她和萊桑德的婚事。他答應讓他們四天後舉行婚禮，也就是在荷米雅原本要被處死的那一天結婚。而海蓮娜所愛的德米崔斯如今變得這麼忠實，她也就滿心歡喜地答應在同一天嫁給他。

P. 65 人們看不見仙王和仙后，但仙王和仙后站在一旁觀看這場大和解。歐伯龍插手幫助，現在看到情人們有了圓滿結局，他們感到很欣慰。善良的仙子們決定盛大舉辦娛樂活動和歡宴，以慶祝即將到來的婚禮。

現在，要是這些仙子的故事和他們的惡作劇讓誰感到不悅，覺得事情太荒誕不可思議，那就當自己是做了一場夢，夢見了這些奇奇怪怪的事。但願我的讀者不會這麼不近人情，竟被一場美麗而無傷大雅的仲夏夜之夢所激怒。

威尼斯商人

P. 76　　在威尼斯有一位叫做賽拉客的猶太人，他是個放高利貸的人，專門借錢給基督徒商人，藉此賺取高額利息，因此積攢了很多財富。賽拉客為人刻薄，借出去的錢錙銖必討，所以善良人家都瞧不起他，有一個叫做安東尼的年輕威尼斯商人尤其討厭他。賽拉客也很痛恨安東尼，因為安東尼常借錢給落難的人，而且不取分毫利息，這位貪婪的猶太人和這位慷慨的商人安東尼，也就因此結下了梁子。安東尼只要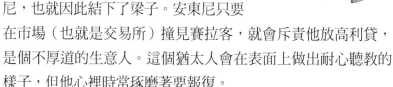在市場（也就是交易所）撞見賽拉客，就會斥責他放高利貸，是個不厚道的生意人。這個猶太人會在表面上做出耐心聽教的樣子，但他心裡時常琢磨著要報復。

P. 78　　安東尼是個好心人，而且他家道殷實，待人謙恭有禮。在義大利，就屬他最能發揚古羅馬的光榮了，所以全城的市民都很喜愛他。他有個好朋友，是一個叫做巴薩紐的威尼斯貴族。巴薩紐的祖產不多，卻有財薄的年輕貴族的毛病，他揮金如土，不自量力，他那一點家產都快被他散盡。而他只要一缺錢用，安東尼就會接濟他，他們看起來簡直是同一條心、同一個錢包。

這一天，巴薩紐來找安東尼，說他想和一位心儀的富家千金成親，藉此也可以改善自己的經濟狀況。這位千金剛剛喪父，是大筆遺產的唯一繼承人。她父親在世時，巴薩紐常去她家串門子，巴薩紐覺得她對自己有意思，似乎有意要他來提親。然而，他沒有資金整修自己的門面來匹配這位富有的繼承人，所以他來求安東尼好人做到底，再借給他三千元。

P. 80 安東尼當時手頭上並沒有錢，不過他想自己有批載貨的船隻很快就會進港，便表示要去找有錢的放高利貸的賽拉客，以押船隻的方式來向他借錢。

安東尼和巴薩紐便一道去找賽拉客。安東尼請猶太人借他三千元，利息隨他開，他會用海上那些船隻所裝載的貨物來還債。

賽拉客聽了之後，心下琢磨道：「要是讓我抓到他的把柄，我就要痛痛快快地把前仇舊恨一次算清楚。他恨我們猶太民族，借錢給別人又不收利息，還在別人面前數落我，罵我正當掙來的錢是高利貸。我要是此仇不報，就詛咒我們猶太人吧！」

他沉思不語，急著用錢的安東尼說：「賽拉客，你聽見了沒？錢你到底借不借？」

P. 82 猶太人聽了答道：「安東尼先生，您三番兩次在市場裡斥喝我借錢放高利貸，我都只是聳聳肩，吞忍了下來，因為受苦是我們的民族性。你又說我是異教徒，是殺人狗，你往我的猶太長袍吐口水，還用腳踢我，把我當成流浪狗一樣。那好了，你現在需要我的幫忙，就跑來找我說：『賽拉客，借錢給我。』狗會有錢嗎？流浪狗借得出三千元嗎？我是不是應該卑躬屈膝地說：『好先生，您上星期三吐我口水，又有一次您說我是

狗，念及這些情分，我
應該借錢給您。』」

安東尼回答：「我還
是有可能再那樣叫你，
或是再吐你口水、再踢
你幾腳。你借我錢，犯
不著當是借錢給朋友，
寧可當是借錢給敵人。
要是我沒錢還，你大可
扳起臉來，按條約行
事。」

「怎麼，看看你！氣
成這樣！我願意和你做

兄弟，得到你的厚愛。我會忘掉你對我的侮辱，你要借多少就
借多少，我半分利息也不要。」賽拉客說。

P. 84　　聽到這個好心的提議，安東尼很驚訝。一副假慈悲的賽拉
客說，他這麼做只是想得到安東尼的友誼，並再度強調他願意
借他三千元，而且不收利息，只要他願意和他去律師那裡簽下
借據玩玩：若屆期未還，當割下身上一磅肉，所割之處，隨賽
拉客之意。

安東尼回答：「好，我就簽了借條，而且我還會說猶太人
的心腸真是好啊。」

P. 85　　巴薩紐認為安東尼不該為他簽下這種借據，但安東尼執意
要簽，他想借約到期之前，他的船隻就會返回，而船上貨物的
價值比債款還高上好幾倍。

賽拉客聽到他們在討論，便喊道：「啊！我父亞伯拉罕，

這些基督徒的疑心病真重！他們自己交易不仁，就懷疑別人的動機。巴薩紐，請你告訴我，要是他未能如期付款，我逼他要那份賠償有什麼用？一磅人肉，從人身上削下來的肉，比羊肉、牛肉都還不值錢，有什麼油水可撈呀。我是為了討好他才賣這份人情，如果他要，那就成交，不然我就送客了。」

猶太人口口聲聲說他是出於好意，但巴薩紐仍不願好友為了他冒這種可怕賠償的險。但安東尼還是不肯聽勸，覺得那不過是鬧著玩的（如那猶太人所說），便簽下了借據。

P.87　　巴薩紐想娶的富有繼承人住在一個叫做背芒特的地方，離威尼斯不遠。她的名字叫做波兒榭，無論是人品或才智，她一點都不輸給我們在書上讀過的那位波兒榭——加圖之女，布魯托之妻。

在好友安東尼冒生命危險給予慷慨的資助之後，巴薩紐帶著一行衣著光鮮的隨從，由一名叫做葛提諾的紳士陪同，前往背芒特。

巴薩紐的求婚過程很順利，波兒榭很快便答應了這門親事。

巴薩紐向波兒榭坦誠自己沒有家產，能夠誇耀的只有自己系出名門，具有貴族血統。波兒榭愛的是巴薩紐的人品，況且她自己家財萬貫，並不在乎夫婿的家業。她優雅謙恭地答道，但願自己能再美個千倍、再富個萬倍，這樣才好匹配他。甚有教養的波兒榭還合宜地謙稱，說自己不學無術，涉世未深，但幸而年紀還輕，尚能學習，凡事都願意虛心受教、蒙他教誨。她表示：

P.88　　「我的人和我的東西現在都歸你了。巴薩紐，我昨天還是這棟豪宅的主人，是自己的女王，是僕人的主人。如今這棟房子、這些僕人和我自己，都歸你了。我就用這枚戒指當作憑藉，獻上一切。」說罷便遞給巴薩紐一枚戒指。

富裕高貴的波兒榭親切地接受了一個家產微薄的丈夫，巴薩紐一方面很感激，一方面也很驚喜。這位親愛的女子如此敬待他，他不知該如何表達喜悅和敬意，只是斷斷續續說了些愛慕和感謝的話。他接過戒指，發誓會永遠戴著戒指，不會拔下來。

葛提諾和波兒榭的貼身侍女涅芮莎，分別在旁侍奉自己的主人和小姐。看到波兒榭這樣得體地答應做巴薩紐的賢妻，葛提諾便向巴薩紐和慷慨的小姐道喜，並要求准允他也能在同時間結婚。

「葛提諾，我打從心底贊成，只要你能找到個妻子。」巴薩紐說。

P. 90　葛提諾這才說，他心上中意的人是波兒榭小姐的美麗侍女涅芮莎，而涅芮莎也允諾過他，只要小姐和巴薩紐成親，她就嫁給他。波兒榭問涅芮莎是否真有此事。

涅芮莎回答：「夫人，若您同意的話，的確如此。」

波兒榭樂而允之。巴薩紐高興地說道：「葛提諾，你們的成親，將讓我們的婚禮更添光彩了。」

這時，這兩對情人歡天喜地的氣氛，卻被一位走進門來的信差給打斷了。他捎來一封安東尼寫來的信，上面寫著駭人的消息。

巴薩紐看著安東尼的信，臉色慘白。波兒榭擔心那封信是通知巴薩紐好友的死訊，便問是什麼消息讓他這麼難過。他回答：「啊，親愛的波兒榭，這張紙上寫著些最悲慘的消息。好夫人，我當初向妳表白情意時，向妳坦承妳我僅有的財富就是我的貴族血統，但我當時應該也要告訴妳，我不僅一文不值，而且還債台高築。」

P. 91　　巴薩紐把我們前面提過的事告訴波兒榭：他向安東尼借錢，安東尼為此跑去跟猶太人賽拉客調錢，簽下借條——如期不還，就用一磅肉來償債。巴薩紐讀安東尼的信，信上寫著：

> 摯友巴薩紐，我的船隻出事了，借據被猶太人扣住。
> 償債之後，吾性命必不保，臨死之前，盼能見君。
> 但唯依君意，若情分不足以請君前來，便莫為此信而來。

P. 92 「哦，親愛的！你盡快把事情安排之後就趕過去吧，你可以用多於二十倍的錢去還債。決不可以因為我的巴薩紐的過失，而讓這位仁慈的好友傷到一根毫髮。既然你是我用這麼高的代價所贖來的，我會格外珍惜你的。」波兒榭說。

波兒榭表示兩人要在巴薩紐動身之前成親，好讓他有權合法使用她的財產。於是當天他們倆就和葛提諾與涅芮莎雙雙完成婚事。婚禮一結束，巴薩紐和葛提諾便急忙趕往威尼斯。當巴薩紐看到安東尼時，安東尼已經鋃鐺入獄了。

還債期限已過，狠心的猶太人不肯收巴薩紐還給他的錢，堅持要安東尼的一磅肉。威尼斯公爵審判這宗驚人案例的日子已經敲定，巴薩紐憂心如焚地等待判決結果。

P. 95 丈夫離行前，波兒榭振奮地和他說話，並囑咐他回來時也要把他那位摯友一道帶回來。然而，她心裡仍擔心安東尼難逃一劫，她獨自思量著是否可以使得上力，去幫忙救出親愛巴薩紐的好友。她願意尊重她的巴薩紐，就像她曾用為人妻子的婉約態度表示說，他比她聰明，她凡事都願聽從丈夫的指示。然而，現在眼見她所敬重的丈夫的好友面臨危險，她就不得不採取行動了。她毫不懷疑自己的本事，單憑她準確完美的判斷力，她當下

便決定親自到威尼斯去為安東尼辯護。

波兒榭有個親戚是個辯護律師，叫做貝拉里。她寫信跟他說明這件案情，尋求他的意見，並請他回信時寄上一套辯護律師的服裝。

P. 97 派去的信差返回時，帶回了貝拉里說明要如何進行辯護的建議，以及所需的裝備。

波兒榭和侍女涅芮莎換上男裝。她套上律師袍，帶著扮成書記的涅芮莎隨行。兩人立即動身出發，在審判日當天趕到了威尼斯。

波兒榭走進元老院這個高等法庭時，案子正當著公爵和威尼斯元老面前即將開審。她遞上貝拉里的信，這個博學的辯護律師在寫給公爵的信裡表示，他原本要親自為安東尼辯護，但因病無法出庭，故請求允許博學的年輕博士包薩澤（他是這麼稱波兒榭的）代他辯護。

公爵一方面批准請求，一面打量著這陌生人的年輕相貌：她披著律師袍，頭上戴著一頂大大的假髮，偽裝得沒有半點破綻。

P. 98 一時重大的審判開始。波兒榭環顧四下，看到狠心的猶太人和巴薩紐，不過巴薩紐沒有認出來喬裝的波兒榭。巴薩紐就站在安東尼的旁邊，他為朋友提心吊膽，焦慮不安。

想到這項艱鉅任務事關重大，波兒榭這婉約女子激出了勇氣。她毫不怯場地執行自己所擔當的職責，她先對賽拉客發言，說明根據威尼斯的法律，他有權索取借據上寫明的賠償。她接著大大說了一番仁慈的美德，任誰聽了都會動容，除了冷血的賽拉客。她說，仁慈就像從天降落到塵世的甘露，是雙倍的福分，保佑施者，也保佑受者。對君王而言，仁慈更勝於王

冠，因為仁慈就是上帝本身的一種屬性。執法時愈是能夠秉持仁慈，這份世俗的權力就愈是接近上帝。她要賽拉客記得我們都祈求上天仁慈，而同樣的禱文也應該教會我們領悟到對待別人也要仁慈。

P. 100　　賽拉客只回答她說，他要索取借據上寫明的賠償。

「他沒有能力還錢嗎？」波兒榭問。

巴薩紐表示，隨便猶太人要幾倍於三千元的錢都可以。但賽拉客不肯，仍堅持要安東尼的一磅肉。巴薩紐乞求博學的年輕辯護律師想辦法稍微變通一下法律，救救安東尼的性命。但波兒榭嚴正地回答，律法一旦訂立，就決不容更改。

聽到波兒榭說法律不得擅改，賽拉客覺得她反倒在為自己辯護，便說道：「但以理再世來審判了！啊，明智的年輕律師！我深深敬仰您！您要比您的外表資深多了！」（譯註：但以理是舊約聖經中具有智慧、善於判斷的人物）

271

波兒楙要賽拉客讓她瞧瞧借據。她看完借據，說道：「就依這張借據做出賠償，這位猶太人依約可以合法索取安東尼心窩處削下的一磅肉。」然後她對賽拉客說：「你還是發發慈悲，把錢收下，讓我把這紙借條撕掉吧。」

P. 102　狠心的賽拉客不肯寬容，他說：「我用我的靈魂發誓，再如何能言善道的人，也不能說動我。」

波兒楙說：「安東尼，既然如此，你的心臟就準備挨刀子吧！」賽拉客興沖沖地磨著長刀準備割肉時，波兒楙對安東尼說：「你有話要說嗎？」

安東尼鎮定豁然地答道，他已經準備就死，無話可說。接著他對巴薩紐說：「巴薩紐，把手給我！再會了！不要因為我為你遭遇劫數就難過。在尊夫人面前為我說好話，告訴她我有多愛你！」

巴薩紐非常沉痛，他答道：「安東尼，我娶了妻子，我視她如自己的性命一般的珍貴，但我這條命、我的妻子和這整個世界，都還不及你的性命珍貴！為了救你，我寧願失去一切，把所有一切都給這個惡徒。」

P. 103 　　聽到丈夫言語激烈地說出對摯友安東尼的愛，善良的姑娘波兒榭雖不以為忤，但仍不禁表示：「要是尊夫人在場，聽了你這番話，諒她不見得會感激你吧！」

　　老愛仿傚主人的葛提諾心想，他總也得學學巴薩紐說段話。此時做書記員打扮的涅芮莎正在波兒榭的一旁做記錄，葛提諾便對她說道：「我有個妻子，我也發誓我愛她，但我希望她就在天堂裡，好請求上帝改變這個狗猶太人的殘忍個性。」

　　「還好你是背著她說出了這個願望，不然你家裡恐怕要雞犬不寧了。」涅芮莎說。

　　賽拉客這會兒不耐煩地嚷著：「我們是在浪費時間，我請求宣布判決。」

P. 104 　　法庭一時之間瀰漫著可怕的預感，每顆心都為安東尼傷痛不已。

　　波兒榭先問秤肉的磅秤是否備妥，然後對猶太人說：「賽拉客，你得找位外科醫生在旁看顧，以免他流血太多致死。」

　　賽拉客的本意就是要讓安東尼失血過多而死，便說道：「借據上並未明載。」

P. 105 　　波兒榭回答：「借據上未寫明又有什麼關係？你做點善事總是好的。」

　　對此賽拉客只是回答：「我看不到借據上有這一條。」

　　波兒榭說：「那麼你可以取安東尼的一磅肉了，法律許可，法庭也批准。你可以割下他胸口上的肉，法律許可，法庭也批准。」

　　賽拉客又喊道：「啊！明智正直的法官！但以理下世審判了！」他磨著長刀，虎視眈眈望著安東尼，說道：「來吧，準備好了！」

「等等，猶太人！還有件一事，這借條上沒有允諾給你血，條文寫的是『一磅肉』。所以你削那磅肉時，只要讓這位基督徒流下半滴血，那你的土地和財產就都要依法沒收充公，歸給威尼斯政府。」波兒榭說。

P. 106 要賽拉客把肉割下而不讓安東尼流血，根本就是天方夜譚嘛。借條上載明的是肉而不是血，波兒榭就憑這一個巧思，救了

安東尼一命。元老院裡響遍了喝采聲，眾人無不讚嘆這位年輕律師的絕妙機智，想出了這麼妙的權宜之計。葛提諾像鸚鵡學舌般地學賽拉客喊道：「啊！明智正直的法官！猶太人，你看看，但以理下世審判了！」

看到自己的毒計無法得逞，賽拉客神情失望地表示願意收下錢。安東尼意外獲救，喜出望外的巴薩紐喊道：「錢在這裡！」

但波兒榭阻止了他，說道：「且慢，不用急。猶太人只能索取所要求的賠償，所以，賽拉客，準備好割那塊肉吧。但是注意不要讓血流出來，而且也不可以少割或多割，只能剛剛好割下一磅。要是少割了或多割了一點點，就不行，如果磅秤顯示的重量有毫髮差距，那就得依威尼斯法律判你極刑，並由元

老院沒收你的全部財產。」

P. 109　　「給我錢，我走！」賽拉客說。

　　「我已經準備好了！在這裡。」巴薩紐說。

　　賽拉客正要伸手拿錢時，波兒樹再度阻止了他，說道：「等等，猶太人，你還有個把柄在我手上。依威尼斯法律，你因為意圖謀害一位威尼斯市民的性命，所以你的財產要充公歸給政府，而你的性命就看公爵是否願意開恩了。你就跪下吧，請求他饒恕你。」

　　公爵於是對賽拉客說：「讓你瞧瞧我們基督徒的精神有什麼不一樣，不用等你開口，我就饒你一命。你的財富半數歸安東尼，半數歸公給政府。」

　　寬宏大量的安東尼接著說，只要賽拉客肯寫下契據，死後將財產留給女兒和女婿，他就願意放棄賽拉客的那一份財產。安東尼知道猶太人有個獨生女，最近不顧他的反對嫁給一個基督徒，對方是安東尼的朋友，叫做勞倫佐。賽拉客為此震怒不已，於是取消了她的財產繼承權。

P. 111　　猶太人答應了這個條件。他復仇不成，財產又被剝奪，便說道：「我人不舒服，讓我回去吧。隨後再把契據送來給我，我會簽字，把我的一半財產留給我女兒。」

　　「那你就回去，但你得先簽字。你要是後悔自己為人殘酷，並改信基督，那政府可寬免你另一半財產的罰鍰。」公爵說。

　　公爵釋放安東尼，宣布退庭。之後，他對年輕律師的足智多謀讚不絕口，並邀他到家裡吃飯。

　　為了比丈夫提前一步回到背芒特，波兒榭答道：「承蒙厚愛，感激不盡，不過我得馬上趕回去。」

　　公爵表示，很可惜他沒空留下來一道吃飯。他轉向安東尼，補了一句說：「好好酬謝這位先生吧，我想這次多虧了他。」

　　公爵和眾元老離開法庭後，巴薩紐對波兒榭說：「最令人敬重的先生呀，多虧了您的機智，我和我的朋友安東尼今天才得以免掉可怕的刑罰。這原本要還給猶太人的三千元，就請您收下吧。」

P. 112　　安東尼說：「您的大恩大德，我們將終身報答。」

　　波兒榭說什麼也不肯接受那筆錢，但巴薩紐仍堅持她應該接受一些報償。她說：「那就把你的手套送給我吧，讓我戴著它做紀念。」待巴薩紐脫下手套後，她瞥見他手指上那枚她送的戒指。原來這位機靈的姑娘是想弄到他的戒指，等之後見到巴薩紐時，可以拿這個來跟他開開玩笑，所以才向他要手套。瞥見這枚戒指後，她說：「承蒙厚愛，那我就拿你這個戒指吧。」

276

巴薩紐很苦惱，律師想要的是他唯一不能離手的東西。他很為難地表示，戒指是妻子所贈，他發過誓要終身戴著，故不便奉送。但他願意張掛榜文，找出威尼斯最珍貴的戒指來送給她。

P. 113　波兒榭一聽，便佯裝受到屈辱。她走出法庭，說道：「先生，你倒是教了我該如何應付乞丐。」

安東尼說：「親愛的巴薩紐，你就把戒指給他吧。看在我的情誼和他幫了這個大忙的份上，就得罪夫人一次吧。」

看到自己這種忘恩負義的樣子，巴薩紐感到慚愧，就讓步了。他派葛提諾帶著戒指去追波兒榭。結果，同樣給過葛提諾戒指的書記涅芮莎，也向他要戒指，葛提諾便一齊奉送出去（他決不讓主人的慷慨專美於前）。

P. 115　兩位姑娘想著，等她們回到家，可以如何地指責丈夫將戒指送出去，並一口咬定是送給哪個女人了。她們想到這裡，不禁笑了出來。

回家路上，波兒榭想著自己做了一件善事，心裡很快樂。她心情愉快，所見的一切都分外美好：今晚的月光前所未有的皎潔，後來賞心悅目的月亮躲進了雲堆裡，這時從背芒特家中所透出的一道光線，讓她奔馳著更加歡樂的想像。她對涅芮莎

說：「我們看到的那道光線是從家中廳堂照出來的，一根小小的蠟燭，竟能照耀得這麼遠。同樣地，在濁世裡，一件善事也夠發出光芒。」聽到從家裡傳來音樂聲，她說：「這音樂聽起來，我覺得比白天的聲音要悅耳多了。」

　　波兒榭和涅芮莎進到家門，換上自己的衣服，等待丈夫回來。不一會兒，丈夫們就帶著安東尼回到家。巴薩紐把他的摯友介紹給波兒榭夫人，她的祝賀歡迎之言尚未說完，他們就看到涅芮莎和丈夫在角落裡吵架。

P. 117　　「怎麼一下子就拌起嘴來了呢？怎麼回事？」波兒榭問。

　　葛提諾回答：「夫人，就為了涅芮莎給我的那個廉價鍍金戒指，上面還刻著刀匠刻在刀子上的那種詩句：愛我，勿棄我。」

　　「詩或戒指代表什麼意義？我給你戒指時，你對我發誓會戴到生命的最後一刻，而你現在卻說你送給律師的書記了。我知道你一定是把它送給別的女人了。」涅芮莎說。

「我舉手發誓，我送給一個年輕人，一個男孩，他個頭小小的，不比妳高。他是那個年輕辯護律師的書記，多虧那位律師的機智辯護，才救了安東尼一命。那個聒噪男孩就跟我要戒指來當作報酬，我說什麼也不能拒絕他啊。」葛提諾回答。

P. 118 波兒榭說：「葛提諾，這就是你的不對了，竟然捨棄妻子所贈送的第一份禮物。我也送給我丈夫巴薩紐一枚戒指，我敢說他無論如何也不會捨棄那枚戒指。」

為了掩飾自己的過失，葛提諾回答道：「就是因為主人巴薩紐把他的戒指送給了那個辯護律師，所以那個辛苦抄寫的書記男孩才會跟我要戒指的。」

一聽到這裡，波兒榭佯裝發怒，責怪巴薩紐把她的戒指送給別人。她說她相信涅芮莎的話，戒指一定是送給了哪個女人。

惹火了自己心愛的夫人，巴薩紐很難過，他懇切地說道：「不，我以人格擔保，戒指不是給別的女人，而是給了一位法學博士。他不肯接受我送的三千元，卻要我的戒指。我不答應他，他就快快不樂地走了。親愛的波兒榭，我能怎麼辦呢？看到自己如此忘恩負義，我很慚愧，只得教人追上去，把戒指送給他。好夫人，原諒我啊。妳當時要是也在場，我想妳會要求我把戒指送給那位可敬的博士。」

P. 119 「哎！你們會吵架，都是因為我的緣故。」安東尼說。

波兒榭請安東尼不要自責，不管如何，他們都很歡迎他。安東尼表示：「為了巴薩紐，我曾經押了自己的身體。多虧妳丈夫送上戒指的那個人，要不然我早就魂歸西天了。我敢再立一張契據，用我的靈魂做抵押，擔保妳丈夫決不會再對妳背信了。」

「那你就當他的保證人吧。把這枚戒指拿給他，叫他可得要更加小心地妥善保存。」波兒榭說。

巴薩紐一看，發現這個戒指和他送出去的一模一樣，不禁吃了一驚。這時波兒榭才告訴他，她就是那個年輕的辯護律師，而涅芮莎就是她的書記。巴薩紐心裡說不出的又驚又喜，原來正是因為妻子卓越的勇氣和智慧，才救了安東尼的一命。

P. 120　波兒榭再一次對安東尼表示歡迎，還把無意中落到她手裡的信交給他。信上寫著，安東尼那批原本以為出事的船隻，都已經安全進港。

就這樣，這位富商故事的悲慘開端，因為出乎意料的好運而讓人遺忘了。他們有的是閒情來笑談戒指的事情，還有兩位不識妻子的丈夫。葛提諾用押韻的話，開心地起誓——

人生在世，唯怕一事，
持涅芮莎的戒指，
誠惶誠恐。

280

皆大歡喜

P. 136 　　在法國還分成若干省分時（當時稱之為公國），有個篡位者廢黜並放逐了正統的公爵兄長，而統治了其中的一省。

　　被逐出自己領地的公爵，帶著忠誠的擁護者退居到椏藤森林。好心腸的公爵和忠誠好友們就在此下寨，好友們為了公爵自願跟著一起流亡，他們不惜拋下領土和稅收，這倒肥了那無恥的篡位者。他們在習慣了森林裡的生活之後，覺得這種逍遙的生活比宮中那種浮華又拘謹的排場自在多了。

P. 137 　　他們住在這裡，好比過著英國羅賓漢一般的生活，每天都會有貴族青年從宮廷來森林裡歸順。山中無甲子，他們像是活在黃金時代裡。夏暑時，他們在林木大樹的涼爽樹蔭下，排排躺著，欣賞野鹿們嬉戲。他們很喜歡這些可憐的斑點傻瓜，牠們才像是森林裡的原住民。為了弄些鹿肉來充飢而不得不殺牠們時，他們還會於心不忍。

P. 138 　　冬天，冷風襲來，公爵感到命運無常。但他安然受之。他說：「這些刮在我身上的凜冽寒風都是忠臣，它們不阿諛諂媚，稟報實情。它們猛烈吹襲，和不仁不義、忘恩負義的那種惡毒完全不一樣。我發現不管如何埋怨逆境，還是可以從中領悟到一些事情，就像可當作珍貴藥材的寶石，原本是從噁心的毒蟾蜍頭上取下來的一樣。」

　　沈得住氣的公爵在看待事情時，總能如此地從中悟出一番寓意。在這遠離人群的生活中，這種喜歡觀物得智的個性，讓他能夠從樹木上得到訓示，從潺潺流水中發現書本，從石頭裡找到教誨，每一件事物都能讓他受益。

P. 140 　　這位被流放的公爵有一個女兒，叫做羅莎琳。篡位者費得烈公爵在放逐她父親時，把她留在宮裡陪伴自己的女兒瑟梨兒。這兩位姑娘情誼深厚，父親之間的嫌隙並沒有影響到兩人的感情。父親行為不義，篡奪了羅莎琳父親的爵位，瑟梨兒為了補償，便竭盡所能地善待羅莎琳。羅莎琳一想到父親被放逐，自己卻仰靠無恥篡位者的鼻息，就覺得很難過，在這種時候，瑟梨兒就會努力安慰她。

　　這一天，瑟梨兒像平時一樣好心地對羅莎琳說：「我求求你，羅莎琳，我親愛的堂姐，請開

心一點。」這時，公爵派來的信差走了進來，通報說有一場角力比賽即將開始，如果她們想看，就立刻趕去宮前廣場。瑟梨兒想讓羅莎琳解悶，便答應要去觀賽。

P. 142　　如今只有鄉下人才會玩角力運動，但在當時，角力是宮廷中最受歡迎的運動，而且還會當著美麗的淑媛和公主面前表演，所以瑟梨兒和羅莎琳也趕往前去觀看。

　　她們想，這次的比賽結果大概會很慘，因為一方是力氣很大的大塊頭，而且他角力運動玩很久了，制服敵手的經驗豐富，然而，這次要和他交手的卻是一個毛頭小子。這個人很年輕，又沒有角力經驗，大家都認為他必死無疑。

　　看到瑟梨兒和羅莎琳前來，公爵說：「女兒、姪女啊，你們怎麼偷偷跑來看角力了？我想是沒什麼看頭的，比賽雙方相差太懸殊了。這小伙子可憐呀，我還想勸他退出這場角力賽呢。兩位姑娘，你們去勸勸他，看能不能勸退他。」

　　兩位姑娘很樂意執行這項人道工作。瑟梨兒率先開口，勸這位年輕的陌生人放棄比賽。羅莎琳很擔心他的安危，也是好心地勸阻他。然而，羅莎琳一番好意的話不但不能讓他打消念頭，反而更讓他一心想逞勇，想在這位可愛的姑娘面前大展身手一番。

P. 144　　他用委婉謙遜的話謝絕了瑟梨兒和羅莎琳的請求，這讓她們更心急。他最後拒絕說：「我很抱歉，未能答應兩位如此美麗動人的姑娘的要求，請讓你們美麗的雙眸和善良的願望，陪我去接受試煉吧。如果我輸了，不過是有個歹命的人丟了臉。如果我被殺了，不過是死了個心甘情願去送死的人。我不會對不起朋友，因為我沒有朋友會來哀悼我。這個世界也不會有什麼損失，因為我一無所有。我在這世上不過是占了個位置，我

把它空出來之後，也許會有更好的人來填補。」

　　這時角力比賽開始。瑟梨兒祈禱這名年輕的陌生人不會受傷，羅莎琳也對他牽掛不已。他說他無親無故，心甘情願去送死，羅莎琳覺得他們同是天涯淪落人，所以對他充滿憐憫之情。看著他比賽角力，羅莎琳很擔心他的安危，簡直像是當下就愛上了他。

　　兩位美麗貴千金的善意，激發了這位無名小子的勇氣和力量。最後他的表現出現奇蹟，竟在終場擊潰對手。對手傷勢慘重，癱在地上，久久都無法開口說話。

P. 146　　看到這個年輕陌生人的勇氣和技能，費得烈公爵很欣賞。他想知道年輕人的姓名和出身，把他收為手下。

　　這個陌生人說他叫歐藍多，是羅藍・德・柏義爵士的小兒子。

歐藍多的父親羅藍‧德‧柏義爵士已經過世多年，他生前是被流放公爵的忠臣和密友。因此，一聽到歐藍多的父親是被流放哥哥的友人，費得烈對這位勇敢年輕人的好感，頓時變成怒氣，逕自忿忿地離開。儘管他討厭聽到任何一個哥哥友人的名字，但他還是欣賞這位年輕人的膽識，因此離開前丟下一句話說，但願歐藍多是別人的兒子。

聽到剛中意上的心上人是父親老友的兒子，羅莎琳很興奮。她對瑟梨兒說：「我父親很喜歡羅藍‧德‧柏義爵士，要是早知道這個年輕人就是他兒子，我會流淚求他不要冒險比賽！」

P. 148　　兩位姑娘走向歐藍多。歐藍多看到公爵突然變臉，覺得困窘不安，她們就跟他說些好話鼓舞他。她們臨走前，羅莎琳回過身，又向父親老友的年輕兒子說了些客氣話，然後從脖子上取下一條鍊子，說道：「先生，看在我的份上，你就戴上這條鍊子吧。我運氣不好，要不然我會送你更珍貴的禮物。」

兩位姑娘獨處時，羅莎琳三句不離歐藍多。瑟梨兒看出堂姐迷戀上了英俊年輕的角力師，她對羅莎琳說：「你會這麼快就墜入情網嗎？」

羅莎琳回答：「我的公爵父親和他父親交情很好。」

瑟梨兒說：「這表示你也應該要愛他兒子嗎？如果是這樣，我就應該討厭他，因為我父親討厭他父親。不過，我並不討厭歐藍多。」

P. 149 看到羅藍‧德‧柏義爵士的兒子，費得烈很不高興，因為這提醒了他，有很多貴族都是被流放公爵的朋友。他早就不喜歡姪女了，她的父親很會做人，所以大家都很同情她。一想到這些，他便對她充滿敵意。就在瑟梨兒和羅莎琳談著歐藍多時，費得烈走進房間裡來。他面有慍色，命令羅莎琳立刻離開宮廷，跟隨他父親一起被放逐。瑟梨兒為羅莎琳求情，但費得烈說，他是為了她才留下羅莎琳。

瑟梨兒說：「我當時並沒有求您讓她留下呀，那時我還很小，不知道她有多好，但我現在知道她的好。我們一直以來都是一起睡覺、起床、讀書、遊戲、吃飯。要是沒有她陪我，我就活不下去。」

費得烈回答：「是你不懂人心啊，她溫順、安靜、有耐心，博取人們的同情。她要是離開了，才能顯出你的聰慧美德，你這樣替她說話，真是傻啊。你不要再替她求情了，驅逐她的判決是不可能收回的。」

P. 151 看到自己沒辦法說動父親讓羅莎琳留下來，瑟梨兒於是毅然決定和羅莎琳一起離開。她當晚就離開父親的宮廷，陪羅莎琳一起去椏藤森林尋找她被流放的公爵父親。

出發之前，瑟梨兒心想，兩個姑娘家穿著一身華麗的服裝上路，安全堪虞，於是就建議兩人喬裝成村姑，隱瞞身分。羅莎琳表示，要是她們兩人能有一人扮成男子，那會更保險。於是兩人很快就做好決定，羅莎琳比較高，那就由她扮成年輕的莊稼漢，由瑟梨兒扮成鄉村姑娘。兩人佯稱是兄妹，羅莎琳說她要化名嘉尼米，瑟梨兒則取名為雅菱娜。

兩位美麗的郡主一番喬裝後，就帶上金錢和細軟當作盤纏，開始漫長的旅程。去榿藤森林的路途遙遠，那裡位在公爵領地的邊界之外。

P. 152　羅莎琳（她現在應該叫做嘉尼米）穿上男裝，英氣煥發。瑟梨兒陪她走過艱辛的好幾里長路，看到瑟梨兒這番堅定的友情，這個新哥哥的精神分外抖擻，好回饋她的真摯情誼。羅莎琳這下真的成了嘉尼米，是溫柔村姑雅菱娜那位純樸而勇敢的哥哥。

最後她們來到榿藤森林，到了這裡，再也看不到之前沿途可見的便利客棧，可以提供像樣的食宿。她們沒有食物，又沒休息，一路上說說笑笑鼓勵妹妹的嘉尼米，這下子也坦承自己很累了，真想乾脆愧對她這一身男裝，像個女人一樣大哭一場。這時雅菱娜也說她走不動了，嘉尼米於是又提醒自己說，女人是弱者，而男人的責任就是勸勉撫慰女人。為了在新妹妹面前展現勇氣，他說：「來吧，雅菱娜妹妹，打起精神。我們路走完了，已經到榿藤森林了。」

P. 154　只是硬裝出來的男子氣概和硬撐起來的勇氣，並無法激勵她們。她們人是到了榿藤森林，但不知從何找起公爵。兩位疲憊姑娘這次的旅程可能以悲劇作結局：她們會迷路，找不到吃的，最後餓死。但天可憐見，就在她們坐在草地上累得半死、求助無門時，一位村民剛好打這兒經過。嘉尼米於是裝出一副莽夫樣，說道：「牧羊人，在這個荒涼的地方，要是憑人情或用金幣可以讓我們換得食物，那就請你帶我們到可以休息的地方。這位

小姑娘是我妹妹，她走得很累了，又找不到吃的，都餓昏了。」

　　村民回答，他是牧羊人的雇工，而他主人的房子就要拍賣，所以他們只有粗茶淡飯，不過如果她們不嫌棄，他們會很歡迎她們一起享用。

P. 156　　於是她們跟著雇工回去，獲救的希望讓她們重新提振了精神。她們買下牧羊人的房子和羊群，並雇用領她們來此牧羊人之家的雇工為僕役。現在，她們很幸運地有了乾淨的茅舍和充足的糧食。她們決定待在此地，直到打聽出公爵住在森林的哪個角落。

　　經過勞頓旅途之後的一番休養，她們開始喜歡上新生活，彷彿真成了所喬裝的牧羊男女。不過嘉尼米不時會想起自己曾經是羅莎琳姑娘，對勇敢的歐藍多一片痴心，因為他是父親友

人羅藍‧德‧柏義爵士的兒子。嘉尼米原以為，她們辛苦跋涉了有多遠，歐藍多就離她有多遠，但沒多久，她就發現歐藍多也來到了椏藤森林。這件離奇的事情是這樣發生的：

歐藍多是羅藍‧德‧柏義爵士的小兒子，爵士臨死時把他（歐藍多當時還很小）交給長兄歐力維照顧。爵士把財產交給歐力維時，囑咐他要給弟弟良好的教育，培育他成為他們這古老家族的榮耀。但歐力維是個不肖的兄長，他不顧父親臨終前的交代，從未送弟弟上學，只是把他留在家裡放牛吃草，無人管教。

P. 158　然而歐藍多的天性和高尚的特質，肖似卓越的父親，所以儘管沒有受過什麼教育，卻活脫像個被悉心教養長大的青年。看到這沒人管教的弟弟外表端莊又舉止高貴，歐力維很嫉妒，甚至加害於他。為此，他派人去慫恿弟弟和知名角力選手摔角，我們之前提過那位選手殺敵眾多。正因這個狠心的哥哥棄他於不顧，所以歐藍多才說他無親無故，想一死了之。

未料天不從惡願，弟弟居然獲勝。歐力維妒恨不已，誓言要放火燒掉歐藍多的寢房。結果這話無意中被父親的老忠僕聽到，老忠僕特別疼愛歐藍多，因為歐藍多長得很像羅藍爵士。

歐藍多從公爵的宮廷裡回來時，這老人迎了出來。他一看到歐藍多，想到親愛的小主人處境危險，不由得激動地喊道：

P. 159　　「啊，善良的主人呀，親愛的主人呀！你讓我想起了老羅藍爵士！你為什麼這麼正直？為什麼如此溫柔、堅強、勇敢？你又為什麼這麼想打敗那個名角力選手？你人還沒到家，名聲就已經先傳回來了。」

　　歐藍多聽了一頭霧水，問他是怎麼一回事。老人告訴他，他那壞心眼的哥哥原本就嫉妒他受到敬愛，現在又聽到他在公爵的宮廷獲勝，聲名大噪，便打算當晚放火燒他的房間，把他燒死。最後他勸歐藍多立刻逃走，亞當（就是這個善良老人的名字）知道歐藍多沒錢。早隨身帶了自己的那一點積蓄。他說：「我這裡有五百克朗，是我在你父親手下做事時，省吃儉用存下來的工錢，準備在我一把老骨頭不能工作時，可以用來當養老金。你拿著，不讓烏鴉餓死的老天，也會眷顧我這老頭子的！錢在這裡，都給你，請讓我當你的僕人吧。我人看起來是老了，但是你有什麼事情和需要，我做起來是不輸給小伙子的。」

P. 160　　「好心的老人家啊！古時候人講的那種忠義，就顯現在你身上！現在世風日下，我們一道走吧，在把你一生的積蓄花光之前，我一定可以想出法子來維持我們兩個人的生活。」歐藍多說。

　　忠僕於是和他心愛的主人一道出發。歐藍多和亞當沒有主意往哪走，他們走著走著，最後來到了樕藤森林。與嘉尼米和雅菱娜一樣，他們在這裡也是苦於無食可覓。他們到處徘徊，尋找人煙。兩人又餓又累，幾乎筋疲力盡。

　　最後亞當說：「啊，親愛的主人，我就要餓死了，我再也走不動了！」他躺下身子，想就地充作墳地，跟親愛的主人訣別。

歐藍多看著老僕人如此虛弱，便抱起他，把他放在舒適一些的樹蔭底下，對他說：「老亞當，振作一點，在這裡歇歇腳吧，不要再說什麼死不死的話了！」

P. 162　歐藍多到處覓食，無意間闖入公爵在森林裡的地盤。此時公爵正和友人準備吃晚餐，這位皇家公爵坐在草地上，除了大樹遮蔭，連個天棚也沒有。

飢餓逼得歐藍多也顧不了那麼多，他拔出劍，想搶奪食物。他說道：「別動，不准再吃，把你們的食物給我！」

公爵問他是落難逼得他這般蠻橫，還是他本來就是個不屑禮節的莽夫。

聽到這話，歐藍多回答說他快餓死了。公爵便邀請他坐下來跟他們一道吃飯。

見他說話這麼和氣，歐藍多收起劍，又想到自己剛剛那種搶奪食物的野蠻行為，臉都羞紅了。

P. 163　「請原諒我，我以為這裡什麼都沒開化，所以才會裝得那麼粗暴蠻橫。不管你們是誰，在這個荒野的淒涼樹蔭下，山中無甲子。如果你們見過好日子，被鐘聲召喚進過教堂，參加過像樣的筵席，如果你們曾經掬過一把淚，懂得憐憫和被人憐憫是怎麼一回事，那麼希望這溫情的話可以感動你們，讓你們用世間的溫情來對待我！」歐藍多說。

P. 164 公爵回答：「我們的確（就像你說的）是見過好日子。我們現在在這荒林裡落腳，但我們也住過城鎮，被鐘聲召喚進過教堂，參加過像樣的筵席，我們也曾因神聖的憐憫心而掬過一把淚。所以你只管坐下，需要多少食物就拿多少吧。」

歐藍多答道：「有個可憐的老人，他一片志誠，跟我一瘸一拐地走了好一段累人的路，衰老和飢餓這雙重虛弱正在折磨他，除非他吃飽了，不然我就唇齒不沾。」

「那就快去找他，把他帶來這裡。我們等你回來再吃。」公爵說。

歐藍多像隻母鹿一樣前去尋找小鹿來餵食。不一會兒，他抱著亞當回來。

公爵見了說道：「把這個可敬的老人放下吧，歡迎你們兩位！」

P. 165 他們餵老人吃東西，幫他振作精神。他復元過來，恢復了健康和體力。

公爵問歐藍多的身分，當他知道他就是老友羅藍・德・柏義爵士的兒子時，就把他留下來照顧。歐藍多和老僕人於是便和公爵一起住在森林裡。

嘉尼米和雅菱娜來到這裡（前面已經提過），買下了牧羊人的茅屋後沒幾天，歐藍多也來到了森林。

嘉尼米和雅菱娜看到樹上刻著「羅莎琳」這個名字，一旁還有十四行情詩，都是寫給羅莎琳的，她們很訝異。就在兩人納悶究竟是怎麼一回事時，正好遇上了歐藍多，她們還看到他脖子上掛著羅莎琳送的那條項鍊。

P. 167　歐藍多沒看出來嘉尼米就是美麗的郡主羅莎琳。她身分高貴，卻紆尊降貴向他示好，讓他不禁為之傾心。他成天在樹上刻下她的名字，寫些十四行詩來讚頌她的美德。現在他看到這位風采翩翩的俊俏牧羊少年，覺得很歡喜，便和他攀談了起來。他覺得嘉尼米長得有點像他心愛的羅莎琳，不過卻沒有那位高貴姑娘的高貴儀表，因為嘉尼米故意表現魯莽，就像個乳臭未乾的小伙子。他調皮詼諧地向歐藍多說，有一個多情的人，「那人在我們的林子裡出沒，在樹皮上刻滿『羅莎琳』這個名字，把我們的樹苗都給糟蹋了。他還在山楂樹上掛起詩句，在荊棘上懸上哀歌，讚美那個羅莎琳。要是我能找到這個多情人，我會幫他出些好主意，讓他不要再害相思了。」

P. 169　歐藍多於是坦承說，他就是那位癡情人，還請嘉尼米透露剛剛提到的好主意。嘉尼米想出的法子和開出的藥方，就是要歐藍多每天來他和妹妹雅菱娜居住的茅屋，他說：「我裝成羅莎琳，你就把我當成羅莎琳來追求我。我會學那些古靈精怪的姑娘對情郎所玩的怪花招，弄得你對自己的痴情都感到好不害臊為止。這就是我說的治療方法。」

歐藍多對這個方法並沒有多大的信心，可是他還是答應每天來嘉尼米的茅屋，玩玩求愛的遊戲。歐藍多天天去找嘉尼米和雅菱娜，把牧羊人嘉尼米當作羅莎琳，天天說些小伙子追求姑娘時喜歡說的甜言蜜語。只是，在治療歐藍多對羅莎琳的痴情方面，並沒什麼進展。

P. 171　　雖然歐藍多覺得這不過是鬧著玩的（他作夢也想不到嘉尼米就是他的羅莎琳），但好歹讓他有機會一吐心曲。嘉尼米也喜歡玩這種祕密的玩笑，他知道這些窩心的情話都是說給她聽的，所以兩人都各自覺得心滿意足。

　　就這樣，這些年輕人度過一段快樂的時光。善良的雅菱娜看到嘉尼米興致高昂，便任由他去，姑且好好欣賞求愛的戲碼，所以也不會費心地去提醒說，她們從歐藍多那裡得知了父親在森林裡的住處，但是公爵父親還不知道羅莎琳在這裡。

　　這天，嘉尼米撞見公爵，兩人聊了一下。公爵問他是什麼出身，嘉尼米回答自己的出身跟他一樣高貴。公爵聽了莞爾，因為他並不認為這個俊秀的牧羊少年會是王室的一員。見到公爵一副健康快樂的樣子，嘉尼米很高興，心想過幾天再跟他做解釋。

P. 172　　一天早上，在歐藍多去找嘉尼米的路上，他看到地上睡了一個人，頸邊還盤踞了一隻綠色大蛇。大蛇一見歐藍多走近，就溜進樹叢。等歐藍多再走近些，又看見一隻母獅子低低地垂著頭，像隻貓一樣蹲守在一旁，等待睡在地上的人醒來（據說獅子不會獵捕死亡或睡著的獵物）。

歐藍多彷彿是老天派來的人，要把這個人從蛇和獅子的口中救出來。然而，當他瞧見這個人的臉，才發現面臨雙重危險的熟睡人，正是待他苛刻又威脅要放火燒死他的親哥哥歐力維。他閃過一個念頭，想任由飢餓的母獅把他吃掉，但手足之情和他的善良天性，讓他放下了憤怒。他拔出劍撲過去，殺死母獅，把哥哥從毒蛇猛獅的口中救出來。然而，歐藍多在撂倒母獅之前，一條手臂被母獅的利爪給抓傷了。

P. 173　　就在歐藍多和母獅搏鬥時，歐力維醒了過來，看到被他狠心虐待的弟弟歐藍多，竟冒著生命危險要從發狂的野獸嘴裡把他救出來，他非常懊悔。他懺悔自己的行為很可恥，涕淚縱橫地請求弟弟原諒他所帶給他的傷害。

P. 174　　看到哥哥這樣懺悔，歐藍多很欣慰，立刻原諒他，和他互相擁抱。歐力維從此真心愛護弟弟歐藍多，即使他原本是打算來森林裡頭追殺他的。

歐藍多手臂上的傷口大量出血，他知道自己虛弱得無法去找嘉尼米，就請哥哥去找嘉尼米，通知他這樁意外。歐藍多說：「我都戲稱他是我的羅莎琳。」

歐力維於是前去找嘉尼米和雅菱娜，告訴他們歐藍多如何救了他一命。待他說完歐藍多的英勇行為和自己幸運逃過一劫的經過後，他才坦承自己就是之前狠心苛待歐藍多的那位哥哥，又表示他們已經和好。

　　歐力維對自己的過錯真心懺悔，善良的雅菱娜看了很感動，不禁對他動了心。而當歐力維在痛說自己的悔過時，看到雅菱娜對他那麼同情，也不禁愛上了她。

P. 175　　愛就這樣悄悄爬進雅菱娜和歐力維的心底，但這時他得忙著照顧嘉尼米，因為嘉尼米一聽到歐藍多遇到危險、被母獅抓傷，就昏了過去。他醒來後，藉口說他是在模仿想像中的羅莎琳昏倒的樣子。嘉尼米對歐力維說：「跟你弟弟歐藍多說，我裝昏倒裝得有多像。」

　　但他一臉蒼白，歐力維看出來他是真的昏了過去。他不明白這個年輕人怎麼這麼虛弱，便說道：「好吧，如果要裝，那就振作些，裝得像個男子漢吧。」

「我也想。不過我應該生做成一個女人才對。」嘉尼米老實回答。

P.177　歐力維離開許久，等他再回來找弟弟時，帶來了好些消息。除了嘉尼米聽到歐藍多受傷就暈厥這件事之外，他也告訴弟弟，自己和美麗的牧羊女雅菱娜墜入情網的經過。他們是第一次見面，但雅菱娜對他的求婚表現出好感。他跟弟弟說他要迎娶雅菱娜，彷彿事情已成定局；他說自己很愛她，願意住在這裡當牧羊人，要把家鄉的莊園和屋舍都讓給歐藍多。

歐藍多回答：「好吧。你們明天就舉行婚禮，我會請公爵和他朋友來參加。去找你的牧羊女，跟她求婚，她現在一個人在家，因為你看，她哥哥來了。」

歐力維便去找雅菱娜，歐藍多則望著前來探望受傷友人的嘉尼米走過來。

P.178　歐藍多和嘉尼米聊著歐力維和雅菱娜的閃電戀情時，歐藍多說，他勸哥哥去說服美麗的牧羊女明天就嫁給他，還說自己多麼希望明天也能夠娶到他的羅莎琳。

嘉尼米很贊成這種安排，他說，要是歐藍多真如他所說的那樣愛羅莎琳，那他的願望就會實現。他明天會安排羅莎琳本人現身，而且那個羅莎琳也會願意嫁給歐藍多。

嘉尼米本來就是羅莎琳姑娘，所以他能輕易讓這樁看起來不可思議的事情實現。但他佯稱假借魔法，還說是從他知名的魔法師叔叔那裡學來的。

聽到這話，痴情人歐藍多半信半疑，他問嘉尼米說的是真是假。

P.180　「我用我的性命作擔保。」嘉尼米說：「穿上你最體面的衣服吧，把公爵和你的朋友都請來參加婚禮。你要是明天就想娶羅莎琳，那她就會來。」

雅菱娜答應歐力維的求婚，兩人隔天早上就來見公爵，歐藍多也陪著一道來。

他們齊聚一堂，準備慶祝這場雙重婚禮。然而新娘卻只有一位，大家看了議論紛紛，以為是嘉尼米在開歐藍多的玩笑。

聽到自己的女兒會奇特地現身，公爵問歐藍多是否相信牧羊少年會實現承諾。就在歐藍多回答他沒有主意時，嘉尼米走了進來。嘉尼米問公爵，要是他把他女兒帶來，他是否會答應讓她嫁給歐藍多。

P. 181 公爵回答：「我會的，就算要拿幾個公國來當嫁妝都可以。」

嘉尼米問歐藍多：「你說要是我把她帶來這裡，你就要娶她？」

歐藍多回答：「是的，即使我是個擁有好幾個公國的君王。」

接著嘉尼米就和雅菱娜一道走開。嘉尼米脫下男裝，重新換上女裝，不需什麼法力，他轉眼間就變成羅莎琳。雅菱娜也脫下村姑的衣服，穿上自己的華服，同樣毫不費力就變成了瑟梨兒姑娘。

在他們兩人離開之際，公爵對歐藍多說，他覺得牧羊人嘉尼米很像他的女兒羅莎琳。歐藍多說，他也看出來兩個人長得很像。

P. 182　　不等他們推測下文，這時羅莎琳和瑟梨兒穿著自己的服裝走了出來。羅莎琳不再佯裝是靠著法力現身，她在父親跟前跪下，請他祝福。

　　她這樣突然出現，在場的人都覺得很神奇，簡直是在變魔法。羅莎琳不想再戲弄父親，便跟他說明自己被放逐的經過，以及喬裝成牧羊人，和假扮妹妹的堂妹瑟梨兒一起住在森林裡的事情。

　　公爵正式批准他允諾過的婚事。歐藍多與羅莎琳，歐力維與瑟梨兒，就在同一個時間結婚了。在這個森林裡慶祝婚禮，雖然沒有一般婚禮的豪華排場，但卻是最快樂的一種婚禮。

　　他們在宜人的樹蔭下享用鹿肉，這時，彷彿為了要使好心的公爵和佳偶們喜上加喜似的，突然來了一為信差，報告公爵一個令人雀躍的消息：他的爵位要歸還給他了。

P. 184　　篡位的公爵因女兒瑟梨兒離家，非常惱怒。又聽說每天都有賢者去椏藤森林投奔被流放的正統公爵，看到落難的哥哥還能受到這般擁戴，他萬分嫉妒，於是率領一支大軍來到森林裡，打算逮捕哥哥，連同他一干忠誠的追隨者一併剷除。但是天意安排得巧妙，竟讓他改變心意，打消了壞念頭。因為壞心眼的弟弟剛進入荒林邊陲時，遇到了一位出家人。那個老人是個隱居士，在跟他一番長談之後，最後讓他打從心底放棄了毒計。

　　從那一刻起，他真心懺悔，決定歸還不當得來的領地，在修道院度過下半輩子。他痛改前非後，首先就派人送信給哥哥（如前面所言），要把他篡奪已久的爵位歸還，讓他復位，而他那些共患難的忠貞追隨者的領地和稅收，也會一併交還。

P. 185　　這個突來的喜訊讓大夥很興奮，而且還來得真是時候，為

兩位郡主的婚禮更添歡樂。羅莎琳的公爵父親時來運轉，瑟梨兒向堂姐道賀，雖然她自己不再是爵位繼承人，仍誠心祝福。羅莎琳的父親復位，繼承人現在變成了羅莎琳，但兩位堂姊妹的感情很好，一點也不會互相妒羨。

對於那些和他一起被流放的忠朋義友，公爵現在終於有機會來報答他們了。那些可敬的追隨者堅忍地和他共患難，如今重返正統公爵的宮廷，享受太平富足，得其所哉。

第十二夜

P. 198　　麥西尼亞的年輕人史裴俊和妹妹菲兒拉是一對雙胞胎（人們認為這是很稀奇的事），兩人生下來就長得很相像，要不是穿著不一樣，根本無法分辨誰是誰。

　　他們在同一個時間出生，也在同一個時間遇險，因為兩人一起坐船出海時，在伊利亞海岸遇到了海難。船在狂風暴雨中撞上暗礁後破裂，只有極少數人倖免於難。

　　倖存的船長和幾個水手坐著小船登陸，菲兒拉也被安全帶上岸。上岸後，這位不幸的姑娘並沒有因獲救而欣喜，而是為遭難的哥哥痛哭。船長安慰她，向她保證說，他在船身裂開時，親眼看到她哥哥把自己綁在堅固的船桅上，他一直都看到他在海上漂浮著。

P. 199　　菲兒拉聽船長這麼說，心裡有了一線希望，便感到寬心多了。這個地方離家很遙遠，她想著該如何在異地安頓自己。她問船長知不知道伊利亞這個地方。

「姑娘呀，伊利亞這地方我很熟。我出生的地方離伊利亞還不到三個小時的路程。」船長答道。

「這個地方是誰的領地？」菲兒拉問。

船長告訴她，統治伊利亞的人叫做歐析諾，他是一位性格和地位都同樣高貴的公爵。

菲兒拉說她曾經聽父親提過歐析諾，那時歐析諾公爵還未成親。

P. 201 「他現在也還沒結婚，起碼最近還沒有。我一個月前離開這裡時，大家都在說他正在追求美麗的奧莉薇（人們總愛談論名人的一舉一動）。奧莉薇是個貞潔女子，她的伯爵父親在一年前過世，改由哥哥來照顧她，但她哥哥不久後也相繼去世。我聽說，為了追思親愛的哥哥，她發誓從今以後不見男性，也不和男性交往。」船長說。

菲兒拉因為痛失哥哥而傷心不已，所以想去投靠這位深切哀悼亡兄的姑娘。她問船長能否帶她去找奧莉薇，她想去當她的僕役。

但船長回答說，這件事不好辦，因為奧莉薇小姐自從哥哥死後，就不准訪客進門，連歐析諾公爵也不行。

P. 202 菲兒拉於是有了另一個想法：她可以換上男裝，去當歐析諾公爵的僮僕。要年輕姑娘穿上男裝、扮成男孩，這個點子有點奇怪，但菲兒拉之所以會這麼想，是可以理解的，因為她這樣一個年輕的美麗女孩如今隻身流落在外，孤苦無依。

她看船長為人正派，好意關心她的幸福，就把自己的想法告訴他。船長聽到之後，馬上答應助她一臂之力。菲兒拉把錢交給船長，請他幫忙買些合適的衣服，並依哥哥史裴俊慣穿的衣服顏色和款式，訂做了衣服。她換上男裝後，看起來和哥哥更是一模一樣了，兩人後來因而被認錯，發生了離奇的誤會。我們後面會談到史裴俊也遇救了。

菲兒拉的這位船長好友，把一位窈窕淑女改造成了一位紳士。菲兒拉化名為夏沙若，船長透過宮廷裡的一些門路，帶她去晉見歐析諾。

P. 204　　公爵很中意這名俊秀少年的談吐和優雅儀態，便收為隨僕，這正是菲兒拉想要得到的職務。這一份新工作她做得盡忠職守，她對主人體貼入微、忠心耿耿，很快地，她就成為公爵最寵愛的侍從。

歐析諾告訴夏沙若自己愛上奧莉薇小姐的來龍去脈。他說，他追求她很久了，可是都沒有結果。他對她獻了這麼久的殷勤，她就是不肯接受。她看不上他，不願見他。自從愛上了這位反應冷淡的姑娘後，高貴的歐析諾連以往喜愛的戶外活動或男性運動都興趣缺缺了。他萎靡懶散，蹉跎光陰，終日只聽那些柔情旋律或激情情歌之類的靡靡之音。他現在疏遠了那些平日多有往來的智臣學士，成天光是和年輕的夏沙若聊天。正經八百的朝臣一致認為，對這位曾經是高貴主子的偉大歐析諾公爵來說，夏沙若決非益友。

P. 206　　由年輕少女來擔任英俊的年輕公爵的知己，本來就是一件危險的事。菲兒拉很快就有了愁緒，歐析諾向她傾訴單戀奧莉薇的苦楚，而她發現自己對公爵也有了暗戀之苦。她最不解的是，這個貴族主子無人能比，任誰見了都會深深景仰，而奧莉薇卻不把他放在眼裡。她壯著膽子，暗示他說，只可惜他愛上了一個不懂得欣賞他的女子。她說：「殿下，要是有位姑娘愛上了您，就像您愛上奧莉薇一樣（或許還真有其人），如果您無法回報那位姑娘的愛，您不也會告訴她，您不能愛她嗎？她不也得接受這個答案嗎？」

　　可是歐析諾不同意這個推論，因為他不認為會有女子能夠像他一樣，如此痴心地愛著一個人。他說，沒有一個姑娘的心房可以裝下這麼多的愛，別的姑娘所能給的愛，無法和他給奧莉薇的愛相提並論。

P. 208　　菲兒拉一向很尊重公爵的看法，但現在她對這一點不以為然，因為她自認她心裡的愛和歐析諾一樣多。她說：「殿下呀，我心裡都明白。」

「夏沙若，你明白什麼？」歐析諾問。

「我很明白女子對男子的愛。」

菲兒拉答道：「我父親有個女兒愛上了一位男子，他們的感情和我們一樣真誠。假如我是個姑娘家，我也可能會愛上殿下您。」

「他們的感情結果如何？」歐析諾問。

「毫無結果，殿下，因為她從來就不表達心意。內心深藏的情感，就像花苞中的蛀蟲一樣，蠶食著她的粉頰。她為情消瘦，臉色蒼白，意氣消沉，猶如一座刻著『忍耐』的石碑，默默地坐在那裡，對著『悲傷』微笑。」菲兒拉回答。

P. 209　　公爵問這位姑娘是否害了相思病而死，菲兒拉回答得很含糊。畢竟這個故事大半是她捏造的，她只是想表達自己對歐析諾的暗戀和黯然神傷而已。

P. 210　　就在這時，公爵派去見奧莉薇的差使走了進來。差使說：「稟告殿下，小姐不肯接見，只叫侍女把她的答覆轉告給您：七年之內，連大自然也見不到她的臉，她要像修女一樣蒙著面紗走路，為了哀悼亡兄，她要把繡房灑滿眼淚。」

聽到這裡，公爵喊道：「啊，她有著那麼美的一顆心。她對亡兄都能這樣念念不忘了，要是哪天愛神的金箭射中了她，她的愛會是何等地熾烈啊！」他對菲兒拉說：「夏沙若，你知道的，我把我的心事都告訴了你，所以，好孩子，你去奧莉薇的家一趟吧。不要吃她的閉門羹，站在她的門口，告訴她，如果她不肯見你，你就會一直站在那裡，直到兩隻腳都長出了根。」

　　「殿下，要是我真和她說話了，您要我說什麼？」菲兒拉問。

P. 212　　「那麼，就把我的情意告訴她，一五一十、完完整整地把我的堅貞愛意告訴她。你是最適合幫我傳達苦戀的人了，你和那些扳著臉孔的人比起來，她會比較接受你。」歐析諾回答。

　　說罷菲兒拉便出發。去勸別的姑娘嫁給自己想嫁的人，這種事她並不樂意做，但既然接下了這個任務，就得忠人之事。不久，奧莉薇就獲報有個小伙子站在門外，堅持非進來見她不可。

　　「我跟他說您病了。他說他知道您病了，所以才要和您談談。我跟他說您睡了，他也好像早就知道了一樣，說正是因為這樣，他更得和您談談。小姐，我要怎麼跟他說？好像怎麼拒絕都沒有用，他不管小姐您願不願意，都非見您不可。」僕人說。

P. 214 奧莉薇對這個蠻橫的差使感到好奇，就吩咐讓他進來。她把臉罩上面紗，表示想再聽聽歐析諾的差使要說什麼。這個差使這麼死纏爛打，她料到準是公爵派來的。

菲兒拉走進門，極力裝出一副男子的模樣。她學大人物的僮僕那套誇飾的宮廷講話方式，對著罩上面紗的小姐說道：「豔光四射、粉妝玉琢、舉世無雙的美人，請告訴我，您就是這府上的小姐嗎？我要是白白把話說給別人聽，那就可惜了，因為這些話不但寫得精彩，而且還是我費了好大工夫才背下來的。」

「大爺，您打哪兒來的？」奧莉薇問。

「除了我熟背的詞，其餘不便多說。這個問題不在我的台詞內。」菲兒拉回答。

「你是個小丑嗎？」奧莉薇問。

P. 216 「不是。」菲兒拉回答：「而且我也不是我所扮演的角色。」這是指她是個女人家，卻扮成了男性。接著她又問了一次奧莉薇是不是這府上的小姐。

奧莉薇回答是。比起替主人傳話，菲兒拉更好奇這位情敵的長相，她急著想看，便說道：「好姑娘，讓我瞧瞧您的臉吧。」

奧莉薇沒有反對這個冒失的要求。這個讓歐析諾公爵追了好久都追不到的高傲美人，卻對夏沙若這個身分卑微的假僮僕一見鍾情。

菲兒拉要求看她的臉時，奧莉薇說：「你的主人是請你來和我的臉談判的嗎？」她一時忘記要蒙面七年的決心，就把面紗拉開，說道：「我還是把簾幕掀開，讓你瞧瞧這幅畫。美嗎？」

P. 218 菲兒拉回答：「您真是天生麗質，雪膚紅頰，巧奪天工。要是您甘心把您的美麗埋進墳裡，不給世間留個副本，那您就是世上最狠心的小姐了。」

「這位大爺呀，我的心沒有這麼狠的。我可以給這個世界寫張單子，列出我的美貌。例如，項目一：兩片朱唇，紅潤相宜；項目二：一雙灰色眼眸，外附眼瞼；還有一圈頸子、一個下巴等等。你是奉命來恭維我的嗎？」奧莉薇回答。

「我知道您這個人了：美麗動人，卻也傲氣凌人。公爵主人愛上了您，對您滿心愛慕。他為您流淚，為愛呻吟嘆息，如雷似火。縱使您艷冠群芳，他理當也該得到回報呀。」菲兒拉回答。

「你家主人很明白我的意思。我知道他的為人，但我就是沒那個意思。我知道他很尊貴，很有地位，正值青春，也很純潔。大家都說他博學、有禮又勇敢，可是我就是無法愛他，這一點他早就應該知道了。」奧莉薇說。

P. 220 菲兒拉說：「要是我也像主人一樣愛您，我會在您門口搭間柳木小屋，呼喊您的名字，寫一些以『奧莉薇』為題的哀歌，在深夜裡高唱。您的名字將會在山中迴盪，我要讓空中那些多嘴多話的回聲一起高喊奧莉薇。啊，你若不眷憐我，您在這天地間就不得安寧了。」

P. 221 「或許你會得逞。你是什麼出身的？」奧莉薇說。

「比現在的身分好，但現在的身分也不算差。我是個紳士。」菲兒拉回答。

奧莉薇一時捨不得打發菲兒拉走。她說：「去找你家的主人，跟他說我無法愛他，叫他不要再派人來了，除非是你回來告訴我他的反應。」

菲兒拉稱她是殘酷美人，然後向她告辭離開。

菲兒拉走了之後，奧莉薇重複著她的話說：比現在的身分好，但現在的身分也不算差。我是個紳士。她大聲說道：「我敢說他是位紳士，他的談吐相貌和舉止氣質，在在都顯示他是一位紳士。」

P. 222 她但願夏沙若就是公爵，她發覺夏沙若已經牢牢抓住自己的心了。她責備自己太快墜入情網，但人們這種溫和的自責總是不夠深切。高貴的奧莉薇小姐和那位假僮僕在地位上的懸殊，還有她那少女的矜持（這是身為一位淑女的主要飾品），一下子就被她拋到腦後，她決定要追求年輕的夏沙若。她派僕人帶上一枚鑽戒前去追他，假裝那是歐析諾送的禮物，夏沙若把它留在她那裡了。

她巧詐地把戒指拿給夏沙若，想藉機透露自己的心意。菲兒拉的確也起了疑心，因為她知道歐析諾根本沒有托她帶什麼戒指。她回想，奧莉薇的神情態度處處都向她流露了愛慕之情，她立刻猜出主人所愛的女子愛上了自己。

「慘了，那可憐的小姐愛上的是一場空夢。我現在明白女扮男裝的危險了，這讓奧莉薇對我空嘆息，就像我對歐析諾空嘆息一樣。」菲兒拉說。

P. 223　　回到歐析諾的宮廷後，菲兒拉向主人稟告此次交涉出師未捷，她重述奧莉薇的咐吩，請公爵不要再去打擾她。

　　但公爵仍寄望斯文的夏沙若早晚會說動奧莉薇來憐惜他，因此要她明日再訪奧莉薇。此際，為了消磨這段煩悶的時光，公爵叫人唱了首他愛聽的歌。他說：「我的好夏沙若，我昨晚聽到這首歌時，心情緩和了不少。夏沙若，你注意聽這首古老而平凡的歌。織女或編織婦坐在陽光下時會唱它，少女用骨針織布時也會唱它。這首歌聽起來是滿無聊的，可是我喜歡，因為它訴說著古時候那種純純的愛。」

歌曲

快來吧，快來吧，死神，
讓我橫陳在淒清的柏木棺材裡。
消散吧，消散吧，氣息，
我死在一位殘酷的美少女手裡。
為我準備插滿紫杉的白色壽衣！
沒有人像我這樣真心為愛而死。
不要半朵鮮花，半朵芬芳的鮮花都不要
撒在我的黑色棺木上：
不要半個朋友，半個朋友也不要來
我的葬身之處，憑弔我悲哀的屍首。
把我埋在癡情人找不到的地方，
省卻千千萬萬回的嘆息與哭泣！

P. 224 　　菲兒拉留意了這首老歌的歌詞。歌詞真切簡單地描繪出單戀之苦，她的神情顯示她感受到了歌曲中所要傳達的情感。歐析諾看到她神情悲傷，便說道：「夏沙若，雖然你還這麼年輕，但我敢用生命來打賭，你已經遇見所愛的人了。對不對呀，孩子？」

P. 225 　　「回稟殿下，多多少少是遇見過了。」菲兒拉答道。

　　「她是什麼樣的女子？芳齡多少？」歐析諾問。

　　「殿下，和您同齡，膚色也和您相仿。」菲兒拉說。聽到這個俊秀的年輕小伙子愛上大自己很多歲的女子，皮膚又和男性一樣黝黑，公爵不禁笑了出來。然而，菲兒拉暗指的是歐析諾，而不是一個長得和他相像的女子。

　　菲兒拉第二次去找奧莉薇時，很順利就見到了她。小姐要是喜歡和年輕俊俏的差使聊天，做僕人的馬上就會察覺到。所以菲兒拉一到，大門就立刻開敞，然後恭恭敬敬地把公爵的僮僕迎進奧莉薇的繡房。每當她告訴奧莉薇，自己再度替主人前來相求時，小姐就會說：「希望你不要再提到他了，不過，要是你想頂替其他人來追求我，我倒願意一聽，而且這還勝於聆聽天籟。」

P. 228　她話講得很白了。不一會兒，她還更加露骨地坦白了自己的愛意，結果卻看到菲兒拉的臉上露出不悅和困惑的表情。她說：「啊，他的嘴角露出輕蔑和憤怒，但那不屑的神情是那麼的美！夏沙若，我用春天的玫瑰、貞操、榮譽、真理向你發誓，我愛你。儘管你很驕傲，可是智慧和理性都無法教我把自己的熱情隱藏起來。」

　　無奈小姐的追求是白費力氣了。菲兒拉連忙離開，揚言再也不會來懇求這位歐析諾所愛的女子。對於奧莉薇的熱烈追求，菲兒拉只用一個決心來回答：決不愛任何女子。

　　菲兒拉一離開小姐後，立刻就有人跑來向菲兒拉挑戰。那個人追求奧莉薇不成，後來得知奧莉薇對公爵的差使有所好感，就跑來下戰書要跟她決鬥。可憐的菲兒拉該怎麼辦？她外表看來是個男子，可是內心裡著實是個女子，她連瞧一瞧自己身上的劍都不敢。

P. 229　看到這個可怕的對手拔劍向她走過來，她開始想承認自己是個女人家。就在此時，來了一個路過的陌生人，讓她不用再害怕，也省了暴露女人家身分所會帶來的尷尬。陌生人一副和她是相識已久的密友一樣，對她的對手說：「這位年輕人如果冒犯了你，那就由我來擔他的不是。如果是你冒犯了他，那

就由我代他來和你較
量。」

菲兒拉還來不及
感謝他拔刀相助，問問
他好心出面調解的原因
時，這位新友人就碰上
了一個讓他英雄無用武
之地的大敵──這時來
了衙吏，衙吏奉公爵之
命來逮捕他，因為他幾
年前犯了個案子。他對
菲兒拉說：「我是為了
找你才被捕的。」他接

著跟她討錢袋，說：「我現在得跟你拿回我的錢袋了。我被捕
了，我很難過不能再為你效力了。看你驚訝的樣子，不過放心
吧。」

P. 231　　　他的話的確讓菲兒拉很驚訝。她表示，她既不認識他，也
沒拿過他的錢袋，但承他好意相助，她就把身上僅有的那筆小
錢拿給他。

　　　結果對方卻口出重話，罵她忘恩負義、冷酷無情。他說：
「你們眼前的這個年輕人，是我從死神的嘴裡把他救出來的。
也是因為他，我才會來到伊利亞，落得這般下場。」

　　　但是官差根本不理會犯人的怨言，只是催他趕快上路，
說：「這我們管不上！」

　　　在他被押走之際，始終一路叫菲兒拉為「史裴俊」，罵這
個冒牌的史裴俊不認朋友。

　　　他匆匆被帶走，菲兒拉來不及問個究竟，但聽到他叫自己是史裴俊，她想他可能是把她誤認成她哥哥了，所以才發生了這種怪事。他說，他曾救過一個人，她但願他救的人就是她的哥哥。

　　　事實的確如此。這個陌生人叫做安東尼，是一名船長。史裴俊在那場暴風雨裡把自己綁在船桅上，在海上漂流。就在他精疲力竭時，安東尼把他救上了船。

　　　安東尼對他萌生友誼，決定不管他上哪裡，都要和他作伴。史裴俊這名年輕人好奇想瞧瞧歐析諾的宮廷，安東尼因為不想和他分開，所以也就來到了伊利亞。可是安東尼知道，自己如果在伊利亞被逮著，就會有生命危險，因為他曾經在一場海上戰役中讓歐析諾公爵的姪子受過重傷。這也就是他現在被捕入獄的原因。

　　　安東尼在遇到菲兒拉之前的數小時，才和史裴俊一道登上了岸。安東尼把錢袋交給史裴俊，要他想買什麼就去買什麼，並表示他出去逛城時，自己會在客棧裡等他。然而到了約定的時間，史裴俊還沒有回來，安東尼便冒險外出找他。因為菲兒拉的穿著長相都和哥哥一模一樣，所以安東尼才拔劍保護他曾經搭救過的年輕人（他以為）。當（他誤認的）史裴俊不認他，又不還他錢袋時，也就難怪他會罵他忘恩負義了。

　　　安東尼走了之後，菲兒拉怕會有人再來下決鬥書，就趕緊溜回家。她走後沒多久，哥哥史裴俊恰巧走來。她那個對手看到他，以為她回來了，就說道：「大爺，怎麼又碰面了？吃我這一招！」說著就給他一拳。

　　　史裴俊可不是懦夫，他加倍回敬他一拳，並拔出劍來。

　　　這時，奧莉薇小姐出來制止了這場決鬥。她把史裴俊誤認

為夏沙若，所以把他請到家裡，並對他所遭到的蠻橫攻擊表示難過。小姐的謙恭和那位不知名對手的粗野，都讓史裴俊很吃驚，但他倒是很樂意到她家裡坐坐。看到夏沙若（她以為他就是）肯接受自己的殷勤，奧莉薇很高興。他們兄妹的長相雖然一模一樣，但她向夏沙若表白時，所不願看到的輕蔑和憤怒表情，在他臉上一點也看不到。

　　史裴俊完全不拒絕這位姑娘的厚愛，他雖然感到莫名其妙，但樂於接受。他想奧莉薇大概是神智不正常，但又看到她是這座華麗房子的女主人，能夠安排事務，把自己的家管理得井井有序。除了突然愛上他這件事情之外，她的腦子似乎都很正常，所以也就樂於接受她的追求。奧莉薇看到夏沙若興致這麼好，很怕他會突然變卦，而家裡這時正好有位牧師在，就提議兩人何不馬上成親。

　　史裴俊答應了這個提議。結婚典禮結束後，他跟夫人短暫告別，打算把他碰到的好運告訴好友安東尼。

　　就在這時，歐析諾來訪奧莉薇。他剛走到奧莉薇的家門前時，衙吏正好押著犯人安東尼來見公爵。因為菲兒拉陪著主子歐析諾前來，安東尼一看到她，就又以為她是史裴俊。他告訴公爵，自己如何從海難中救了這個小伙子一命。當他說完如何真心善待史裴俊之後，他抱怨說，這三個月來，他都和這個不知圖報的小伙子朝夕相處在一起。

　　這時，奧莉薇小姐從家裡走出來，公爵無心再聽安東尼的故事。他說：「伯爵小姐來了，天仙下凡了！至於你這傢伙，瘋言瘋語的。這三個月以來，這小伙子一直侍候著我。」說完就命人把安東尼帶開。

　　然而，歐析諾視為天仙的伯爵小姐，很快就讓公爵指責起夏沙若忘恩負義，一如安東尼那樣，因為公爵聽到的都是奧莉薇對夏沙若的滿嘴好話。看到自己的僮僕這麼受奧莉薇的青睞，他揚言要菲兒拉得到她應得的可怕報復。離去之際，他要菲兒拉跟他走，並且說道：「走，孩子，跟我走，我要好好痛懲你一頓。」

　　歐析諾妒火中燒，菲兒拉眼見要被處死，但愛情讓她不再膽怯。她說，為了安撫主人，她願意死。

　　但奧莉薇不想失去丈夫，她喊道：「我的夏沙若要去哪裡？」

　　菲兒拉回答：「我要跟他走，我愛他，他比我自己的命還重要。」

　　奧莉薇不讓他們走，她大聲宣布夏沙若是她的丈夫。她請出牧師，牧師說，他為奧莉薇小姐和這名年輕人證婚還不到兩個小時。菲兒拉極力否認和奧莉薇成過親，但在奧莉薇和牧師的作證之下，歐析諾認定了僮僕橫刀奪走了他看得比自己性命都還珍貴的寶貝。

P. 240 如今事情走到了這般田地，歐析諾只好跟這位不忠的情人和那個小騙子丈夫菲兒拉道別，並警告菲兒拉永遠不要再出現在他眼前。就在此時，（他們這麼認為）不可思議的事情發生了——走來了另一位夏沙若，還稱奧莉薇為妻子。

這個後來出現的夏沙若就是史裴俊，他才是奧莉薇的正牌丈夫。大夥看到這兩個人的長相、聲音和服裝都一模一樣，一陣驚訝之後，兄妹倆開始詢問對方。菲兒拉不敢相信哥哥還活著，史裴俊也不明白他以為已經溺斃的妹妹，怎麼會穿著年輕的男裝出現。喬裝過的菲兒拉隨即承認自己就是妹妹菲兒拉。

因孿生兄妹長相酷似而引起的一切誤會都澄清之後，大家

又笑奧莉薇小姐擺烏龍地愛上了一個女人家。不過，知道自己嫁的是哥哥而不是妹妹時，她倒也不討厭這種對調。

P. 242 奧莉薇已經結婚，歐析諾美夢幻滅。這份沒有結果的愛，隨著希望的落空而消逝。現在，他的心思倒是都放在年輕寵臣夏沙若變成窈窕淑女的這件事情上。

他仔細端詳菲兒拉，他沒忘記自己一直就覺得夏沙若長得很俊俏，相信她穿上女裝一定會非常美麗動人。他也沒忘記她老是說「她愛他」。當時，那聽來只不過是忠實僕僮的份內話，可是現在他猜出必有弦外之音，她跟他說的那些好聽話，有很多都像是在打啞謎。這下他總算恍然大悟了。回想起這一切之後，他當下決定要娶菲兒拉為妻。他對她說（他還是忍不住叫她夏沙若或「孩子」）：「孩子，妳跟我說過上千次了，說妳對女人的愛，永遠比不上對我的愛。妳接受的是女子的溫柔教養，卻忠心為我做了這麼多事，又叫我是主人叫了這麼久，所以妳現在就做主人的夫人，成為歐析諾真正的公爵夫人吧。」

P. 245 奧莉薇本來就不接受歐析諾的感情，如今看到他把心獻給了菲兒拉，就邀他們進到屋子裡，表示要請早上才為

她和史裴俊證婚的牧師幫忙，也在當天為歐析諾和菲兒拉主持婚禮。

就這樣，這對孿生兄妹雙雙在同一天結了婚。那場拆散他們的暴風雨和船難，如今卻促成了他們這等傲人的好運氣。菲兒拉成了伊利亞公爵歐析諾的妻子，而史裴俊也娶了富裕高貴的伯爵小姐奧莉薇。

悅讀
莎士比亞
四大喜劇故事

仲夏夜之夢
威尼斯商人
皆大歡喜
第十二夜

作者 _ Charles and Mary Lamb

前言／導讀 _ 陳敬旻

編輯 _ 安卡斯

校對 _ 陳慧莉

封面設計 _ 林書玉

製程管理 _ 洪巧玲

發行人 _ 周均亮

出版者 _ 寂天文化事業股份有限公司

電話 _ +886-2-2365-9739

傳真 _ +886-2-2365-9835

網址 _ www.icosmos.com.tw

讀者服務 _ onlineservice@icosmos.com.tw

出版日期 _ 2018年10月 初版一刷（250101）

郵撥帳號 _ 1998620-0 寂天文化事業股份有限公司

國家圖書館出版品預行編目資料

悅讀莎士比亞四大喜劇故事 / Charles and
Mary Lamb 著；一初版. 一[臺北市]：寂天
文化, 2018.10 面；公分. 中英對照

ISBN 978-986-318-735-6 (平裝附光碟片)
　　1. 英語　2. 讀本

805.18
107015704